Dragon Steel

A Finely Aged Book

Jodi Kendrick

SoulGate Publishing

Jodi Kendrick

Romance. Adventure. Passion.

Dragon Island
Dragon Heat

Enchanted Ardor
Wish

EveL Worlds : FUCN'A
Tough Nut
Diamond in the Ruff
Honeyed Nut
Gorilla in the Hiss
FUCN'A Collection One
Pedigree Collection

Finely Aged
Dragon Steel

Global Paranormal Security Agency
Awakened
Surfacing
Polestar
Aquatic Investigations
Prowler

The Kindred Chronicles
Healer
Mercenary

The Soaring Dragon Chronicles
Return Flight
Changeling

Welcome to Dragon Island

A hidden archipelago in the Bermuda Triangle, Aeleftheria Nisi is a thriving community of female dragon shifters and a few humans that live independently of any males.

In fact, they're not welcome.

Centuries ago, the Queen and her council decided to break away from the domineering rule of the male dragons to govern themselves.

Some of the male dragon tribes are determined to bring the females back under their control.

The females will fight to the death to ensure their sovereignty.

Acknowledgments

Thank you!
To my family, friends and writing community. Your continued love, support and encouragement keep me going. Without you, I'd still be dabbling and drifting.

Jess, thanks for ALL the things in this whirlwind you've instigated!

Kim, thank you for all the work you do to make my words make sense!

John & Kevin, thank you for helping me plug plot holes and hammer out character bumps.

My deep appreciation goes out to **Milly Taiden** for her generosity in opening her creative worlds to those of us that enjoyed playing in them!

For Deb.

Chapter 1

KOLINA STEELSCALE STOOD ON the tower platform overlooking the island of Aeleftheria Nisi spread out before her. A collection of villages lay strung along the coastline, stretching inland and joining, until one city nestled against the base of the queen's citadel.

Dragon shifters and humans alike, all female, living and working together, maintaining the harmony of the archipelago civilization hidden in the vast Atlantic Ocean, deep in the region known to the rest of the world as the Bermuda Triangle.

She stood, hands resting behind her back with her fingers curled around a locket, feet planted shoulder-width apart, monitoring the comings and goings below, as well as the increased patrol progress above. Swallowing a lump in her throat, she straightened her spine, pushing away intrusive thoughts of her daughter.

That will do you no good, Kolina.

Three dark spots in the sky approached in a uniform arc, growing larger until Kolina could make out the shape of their wings, supporting their glittering scale-covered bodies through the air.

She rubbed a thumb over the etched surface of the locket in her grasp once more before tucking it into her pocket. She used the few seconds before they landed to tie her long, graying, dark hair back from her face.

They came in fast, and banked hard, pushing the air into chaotic eddies of turbulence that twisted across the open deck of the platform. Kolina closed her eyes against the kick-up of dust, but not before she caught the flash of color adorning the claws of the left-wing guardian.

The currents settled. She opened her eyes and raised a brow, but otherwise waited patiently for the three to land, shift from their dragon to human form, and grab their robes from the change room.

"Aunt Kolina," the one approaching addressed her.

Kolina looked pointedly at the color glittering on her finger and toenails, visible above her open-toed sandals. "I thought you and Kymri didn't get along."

Zayli snorted. "Cousin-rivalry. We may not get along *all* the time, but we're still kin." Besides, I miss her, and nail polish is her thing."

"You miss pushing her buttons," Kolina said, turning to walk along the parapet and not toward the inner guardian offices. "I suppose some of the others aren't making it easy for you?"

Zayli shrugged. "I ignore it." She followed Kolina around toward another platform on the south side of the tower.

"How is it out there?"

"You've read the reports."

Kolina nodded. "And?"

Zayli sighed. "It's storm season, so everyone's exhausted with the extra patrol duty. Tempers are flaring more than usual. I'm not telling you anything you don't already know, or anything more than I report to my commander. Why are you here?"

Kolina stopped walking at the blunt question.

"Has Marli returned to the island, or has anyone left to meet with her and Kymri?"

Zayli shook her head. "No one would dare, without Queen Regina's permission or command. What's going on?" She dropped her voice.

Kolina drew a deep breath, debating what to say to her niece—if anything at all. After a moment, she looked back toward the horizon and blew out a breath. "I don't know. At least, not yet."

"But something's wrong?" Zayli straightened, alert. "I haven't seen you concerned in a long time."

Kolina nodded. It wasn't something she could put a finger—or a claw—to. Not yet. It was a pitched vibration almost unnoticed. Almost. Like a dog whistle. Inaudible, but at the right pitch to slide under her scales and ride the nape of her neck.

"If you *feel* something, you'll tell me. Report it to your commander, of course, but report to me too. *Anything* out of place. Your commander won't ask it of the guardians under her orders. It isn't her style. But I want every dragoness, of every squad, reporting what they can't see, hear, taste or smell, too."

Zayli frowned. "Yes, aunt."

Kolina sighed and softened a fraction, reaching out her hand to touch her niece's shoulder; something that before Kymri's absence, she'd have never done.

Things had changed.

"I know there is a lot of tension between everyone. Between you and others, because of Kymri. Our duty to our queen's safety is above that."

Zayli snorted. "You don't have to tell *me* that. I know all about duty." She did nothing to mask the acid in her tone.

Kolina nodded.

Zayli was the one that always pushed the 'duty' line and had been right there supporting Kolina when she'd talked to Kymri about hers. "Is that all, Aunt?"

"Yes. Thank you."

Zayli turned at the next open archway leading toward the interior of the tower and strode down it in the direction of her quarters.

Offspring.

It was the one area of Kymri's life that she'd refused to fulfill.

And now, the long-standing peaceful island was struggling to keep from slipping into chaos.

Kymri's resistance to her duty to have young had pushed her into a heat that resulted in poor judgment choices.

Kolina sighed. She couldn't blame Kymri for the recent attacks from the male dragon tribe, but everyone else did. The object of her heat, Jori Mountainside, had unknowingly led them right to the island, threatening the safety of both the queen and the rest of the population.

Now, they were all on high alert to fend off more attacks from the much larger dragons.

More would come.

They all knew it.

And there'd been no more information from Kymri or Marli since Marli's sparse report arrived from the continent.

All they knew was that Kymri and Jori were alive, as was Elora—Jori's mother and the queen's trusted ambassador—who'd disappeared several decades before, and that the Dragon King was dead.

But that wouldn't stop his radicalized followers from carrying on his ideology and attacking the female-populated island to take control.

None of them would allow that to happen, but given how much larger male dragons were than female—it wouldn't be easy. The queen's guardians were all highly trained warriors. They'd die for their queen and people.

Why hasn't Kymri come back?

Kolina stepped into the frame of her long-time friend Launia's open office door.

Launia glanced up from the reports she scowled over, lips quirking at the corners. "I wondered how long before you graced my threshold."

"Well, you know, the queen likes to keep me busy." She brushed the hair from her face, tilting her nose toward the ceiling.

Launia snorted at Kolina's affectation of self-importance, reminding both of them of some of their island sorority. Her eyes twinkled, and the severity of the worry lines creasing her forehead eased. Then she raised a brow. "Are you here officially, or personally?"

"Both." Kolina closed the office door and approached Launia's desk, resting a haunch on the corner as she looked down at her friend and colleague.

Launia eased back in her seat, folding her hands across her lap as she eyed Kolina. "Reports are unchanged. The guardians are exhausted."

Kolina nodded. "I spoke to Zayli." She repeated what she asked of Zayli.

Launia's gaze narrowed on Kolina, worrying a lip as she considered her request.

"That bad, huh?"

"Maybe. That's the problem. I just don't know. The queen has been...different, since Kymri left. Everything feels different."

"Or you're not sleeping enough and are worrying about your youngling."

"Who isn't so young anymore. Not for a long time."

Launia snorted again, brow rising higher as she studied Kolina again.

Kolina sighed. "I know. You don't have to say it." Kolina knew full well how much she had interfered in Kymri's life.

And she was sure that was the reason Kymri had re-sisted her duty to produce offspring for so long, until her biology hadn't given her a choice.

Kymri: Independent, stubborn, loyal.

Gone.

For weeks now.

She stood, pacing the length of Launia's heavy, ornately carved wood desk. "This is all my fault. If I hadn't pushed Kymri so hard, she'd still be here, carrying her child in the safety of our island home, the male dragon tribe never having found us."

"Don't do that. Kolina, we all knew they'd find us one day. It was always just a matter of when. And Jori Mountainside's arrival would have happened regardless of any family squabbles between you and your daughter."

Kolina abruptly changed topics. "I can't believe Elora is alive."

Launia blinked, nodding. "And Odson never said a word about it. Maybe that's why the queen is unsettled."

Kolina's gaze darted back to Launia's face, heart twisting in her chest. "Odson Blackridge has always been a wild card." She considered the circumstances of his withholding that information for so long. "But I understand why he kept that secret from her—why Elora asked it of him."

Kolina knew too well what it was to have to make hard choices to protect a son, unwanted by their society.

Many of the dragonesses on this island did.

After Kolina left Launia's office, she walked the circumference of the island, studying the walled citadel, with its towers stretched skyward, looking for flaws in their defenses from below. The Queen's Spire soared above all the others, a beacon of the queen's presence on the island. The city surrounded the walls like a layered cloak down toward the uneven shoreline. Sailing ships buoyed in the harbor, fishing boats lined the smaller keys and docks.

Everything looked as it should.

And yet, Kolina couldn't shake her unease.

Was it just the effects of recent events and the revelation that the queen's longtime companion, Elora, was in fact still alive, after her disappearance from a diplomatic mission more than three decades ago?

Kolina extracted her locket from her pocket again, wrapping the chain over her fingers as she studied the etched surface. Its finely crafted face bore the insignia of an elite Aeleftherian guardian commander.

Its existence was shrouded from others most of the time. It usually lay out of sight, against her chest, under her clothing. Since events with Kymri and Jori, Kolina found herself reaching for it more and more, seeking the comfort of its solidity in her hands; what it represented.

Her thumb slipped over the image of the winged shield once more before she fastened the delicate chain's clasps behind her neck and tucked it back under her shirt.

With a sigh, she cast her gaze back across the horizon.

If the queen were deeply unsettled, the resonance of her magic could create the sense of island-wide unease.

But if there was something else, something dangerous causing it, then Kolina had to figure out what it was.

As a member of the Queen's Honor Guard, it was her duty to ensure the safety of their monarch, which ensured the safety of their small nation.

She surveyed the harbor. None of the ships were unfamiliar. The port master did her job as diligently as everyone else under the queen's rule.

Every dragoness that chose to live on the island did so with the full understanding of the queen's absolute rule and accepted the established laws for the protection of the tribe.

No one wanted to go back to life under the dominance of the male tribe.

No one.

Anyone that disagreed with the laws, left.

It had been more complicated than that for Elora. The queen's closest companion and loyal ambassador. She hadn't left the island with the purpose of abandoning her people. Just the opposite. She just hadn't come back.

Kolina had been in the queen's chambers during Odson Blackridge's retelling of Elora's story up to the point of her supposed second disappearance. What she'd endured in the claws of the Dragon King. And yet, she'd never given away the island's location to *him*.

But she had to her son. Covertly, yes. But she'd still given them that information.

Something Kolina had never done.

Her thoughts briefly flicked to the past, hit a wall of heartache and bounced back to the present. Her fingers brushed against the fabric of her shirt over the locket.

I need to fly.

She climbed back up to the nearest citadel gate and up higher still to the flight platforms.

Another rotation of guardians arrived and departed.

Near the platform jutting from the Queen's Tower, where her personal guard resided, Kolina stripped in the change room and made her way out to the ledge.

Several of her fellow Queen's Guard eyed her, their judgment plain on their faces.

Drawing her magic inward, the air around her shimmered and writhed. Her consciousness remained focused on the change as her body mass expanded until she stood on thick-padded talons. The metallic scales of her forelegs glittered under the tropical sun. Her body shimmered as she launched. Her wings snapped out and down, forcing her upward before they curled inward and pushed down again. And again, until she caught the higher currents, through gradient layers of blue sky.

Her shoulders settled with the old familiarity of the archipelago patrol route.

When Kymri was old enough to join the guardian patrols, Kolina had moved into her own mother's position in the Queen's Guard while her mother had stepped into the Queen's Council.

It was the way of things.

Kymri.

Would she come back? Surely, she would bring her youngling back to the island.

I've pushed her away.

She had bonded with Jori Mountainside. That changed everything. Complicated things beyond a simple heat.

A bond.

Kolina flew higher.

The patrols were visible off her wingtip. She wouldn't interrupt them.

She soared toward the small island at the farthest end of Draconia's archipelago, where Kymri had found Jori and his little plane, throwing everyone's lives into turmoil.

Find her.

Angling her nose toward the main island, she rode the currents home.

She had to review the transcripts of Marli's report.

A deep base tone rippled out from the citadel.

Every muscle in Kolina's body tensed, her head whipping in the direction of the sound.

An attack!

She slid her gaze across the vast horizon looking for the source of the threat.

There!

North of the island, a cluster of dark specks swarmed around itself.

Bringing her wings down with a hard push, she climbed the atmosphere, gaining height, and then speed when she angled herself and tilted her wings, turning herself into a giant snarling arrow.

Two attackers were being harried by three patrol guardians. Three wasn't enough, but more were coming.

One of the larger male dragons broke away from the cluster, angling downward, claws extended, toward the island. Not toward the citadel. The villages.

Kolina's heart leaped into her long throat. She knew every woman and child in those villages. She was close enough now to see them scurrying between the houses and shops seeking shelter. Most streamed toward the citadel. Others would go into their cellars or find other hiding places, but there wasn't enough time for everyone to find adequate shelter from a dragon, let alone a male dragon.

More guardians moved to intercept him, but not in time to stop him from razing a few small houses.

Kolina tilted, pulling her wings in tight, and dove. Holding her breath, she plunged faster and faster.

She roared, drawing the attention of the guardians attacking the destructive male, just in time for them to pull away. She adjusted her angle in the last seconds, colliding with him so hard the impact sent them both soaring back out toward the ocean.

The hit knocked the breath from her. Pain streaked through her shoulder, sharp and blinding. She held her focus long enough to get her claws into him so that the weight and momentum of her body would force him down into the water before his shock wore off.

In the water, she would be just as vulnerable. As soon as they stopped sinking, she pushed off from him, swimming to the surface before he could turn her tactics back on her.

His teeth grazed her tail from below.

She swung it, snapping him in the face with its tip, as she continued to force her way upward.

He lunged again, sinking his teeth into a thicker part of her tail. Her hind leg kicked out, claws tearing into his face, forcing him to release her.

Her head broke the surface and she dragged air into her lungs while using her forearms and hindquarters to propel herself toward shallow water so she could get back into the air. Pain spiked through her left shoulder with each movement.

Clouds of blood drifted through the ocean water around her. She couldn't tell if it was his or her own. She didn't care.

Guardians circled overhead, waiting for the male to reappear. The other male now had eight harrying guardians forcing him away from the island, their jaws snapping at him, trying to catch a wing or his tail, to force him down too.

Finally reaching the land shelf several miles down the shoreline from the closest village, she struggled to get back into the air. Pain flared through her shoulder when she flexed her wings.

Dragonsdammit!

Overhead, her sisters battled. Attack, counterattack, blocking the male's attempts to do more damage to the island and Aeleftheria's inhabitants.

They aren't taking anyone. They're here to destroy us.

The male she'd brought down into the water swam toward the smaller islands. His own cluster of guardians circled overhead, tracking his progress.

Her tail throbbed where his teeth had crushed through some of her scales and punctured her hide. Favoring her left foreleg, she limped to shore, her eyes on the action above.

The longer she stayed in her dragon form, the faster she would heal, but the pain made it difficult to hold the magic. The human part of her wanted to retreat into darkness, allowing oblivion to soothe the wounds. She stubbornly held her form, watching and listening with her keener dragon senses until the combatants were nothing more than swirling specks in the sky. Muted roars continued to roll across the surface of the ocean until they were indistinguishable from the waves crashing into the shoreline.

Still, she waited, in case they came back.

They didn't return.

She limped her way closer to the nearest village.

Finally, the guardian squads returned. One dragoness broke away from her small cluster.

Zayli.

Kolina let go of her magic, shrinking down to her human form. Her lower back throbbed, her shoulder screamed.

Zayli landed, then angled her wing to make room for Kolina to ride. She huffed impatiently.

Kolina was in too much pain, and too old, to let pride force her into a naked, head-held-high stroll back through the villages and up to the citadel to present herself to the shamans.

She struggled to climb her niece's foreleg to settle precariously on her back, clinging to her spikes without impaling herself. The trip took minutes.

Kolina slid off Zayli's neck into the care of several waiting shamans on the patrol platform closest to the infirmary.

Chapter 2

Several days after the attack, Kolina sat at her desk, reviewing the transcripts of Marli's report.

Launia appeared in the open doorway and said, "Summons from the queen." Approaching the desk, she extended a white card to Kolina.

"Thank you." Kolina rose, accepting the card. She read it with a glance then went to the cupboard that held her official robes. Donning them, she followed Launia back into the corridor.

"How is your shoulder?"

Kolina grimaced. "Inconvenient."

"And probably sore as hell. I'll catch up with you later," Launia said before she disappeared at the next junction.

Kolina continued on, her footfalls echoing off the ancient stone floor and walls. At her destination, she raised her head so that her eyes were level with the dragon carvings adorning the heavy wooden door to the queen's chamber. The spear-armed guard to the right opened the door for her to pass through. It hushed closed behind her.

The queen occupied the ornate chair at the head of the room and her inner council occupied the chairs surrounding the massive oak table.

Kolina's mother, a matron with silvered hair pulled back into a severe braided bun, held her gaze. She gave nothing of the purpose of the meeting away in her expression. Kolina avoided assessing the faces of the other councilors. They would be equally as impassive, or heavily scornful.

No matter.

Kolina turned her attention to their queen and bowed. "Honor Guardian Steelscale. Welcome."

Kolina straightened, clasped her hands behind her back, feet spread to shoulder width.

She waited.

Kolina controlled her breathing beneath the weight of the queen's assessment.

Finally, the queen spoke. "Adjourned."

There was another heartbeat of silence before the room filled with the quiet scraping of chairs and rustle of robes as the Council vacated the chamber.

Still, Kolina kept her eyes on the queen, but she felt the weight of judgment from the others as they left her alone with their sovereign.

They blamed her, as they blamed her daughter, for the recent turn of events.

If she'd counseled her daughter properly in her duties—if she'd done more to divert Kymri's rebellious ways, the island and their queen would be safe.

But she hadn't, and they weren't safe.

As soon as the door closed behind them, the queen stood, gliding toward the sideboard which held crystal cut decanters and glasses. She set two glasses upright and poured the sapphire blue liquid into both and gave them a swirl before approaching Kolina, handing one to her.

"I want you to leave the island."

Kolina's heart stopped. She nearly dropped the glass the queen had just set in her grasp. She stared down at the swirling blue alcohol clutched in her palm. It was fermented from a berry grown only on their island chain. The queen's special drink. Usually reserved for the closest of friends or most dangerous allies.

Waiting for the queen to elaborate, she drew a slow, even breath, willing her heart to restart.

Her Majesty enjoyed a little drama and theatrics.

Finally, Kolina looked up, meeting the queen's mirth-filled face. Her eyes twinkled with mischief over the rim of her glass as she sipped.

Whatever she was going to say, the Council didn't like it—or *wouldn't* like it.

Kolina sipped the liquor. Hot and smooth, it slid over her tongue and warmed her chest and belly on its way down, fortifying her for whatever the queen was plotting.

"I want to know what's going on. With your daughter. With Elora. How the king is suddenly dead, and why. I want you to bring them home."

Kolina blinked.

"I'm Queen's Guard. My duty is here, Your Majesty. We're anticipating more attacks."

The queen waved a hand. "We're always anticipating attacks. And don't tell me what my council has just told me. I'm aware the defense of my person and of the citadel is vital." She knocked back the rest of her drink. "I hate sitting here blind when there's been a sudden and wholly unexpected upheaval—especially among the male tribe. I need a spy."

They had spies in the field.

"Marli would get far more reliable information from Kymri than I would."

The queen considered this. "She's a good guardian and I trust her. But in this, I trust you more, Kolina. You *understand* what's at stake."

She did. It was a delicate situation.

They were both mothers of children they'd had to give up for the good of the island.

Male children.

At the immovable insistence of the Council.

A situation Elora faced three decades ago.

A situation Kymri may have to face months from now.

"I've already reviewed the transcripts of the report Marli sent—which held very little in terms of useful content."

"Which is why she's remaining in the field, and I need you to go out and collect more information."

"I'll prepare to journey to Black River first and seek Odson Blackridge's aid. He must know where they are by now."

"Good. There's a ship leaving in the morning. I have some things I want you to take. I want you to give Heidi

Brandt a bottle of my Sapphire wine when you arrive at Black River, along with an invitation to visit."

I hate sailing.

Unfortunately, her injured shoulder meant that she couldn't fly yet.

Kolina drained the last of the wine from her glass in a final swallow.

Her eyes flicked back to her sovereign, who observed her with a weighted stare.

"Yes, Your Majesty."

The queen's lips lifted at their corners. "Good. Give Heidi my love and put all your charm into that invitation."

Kolina lifted a brow. "Charm?"

"I know you have some, Kolina. You just need to relax a little." The queen winked and waved Kolina away in dismissal.

CLIVE'S FACE BURNED, BLINDED in one eye. He ached all over. And he was pissed as all hell. More pissed than when they had set out to 'visit' Aeleftheria Nisi.

He glanced at Merwin, flying off his right wing. He looked as bad as Clive felt.

Those little bitch dragonesses had shredded them. Again.

There were too many for the two of them to handle by themselves. He could handle a few, but more than that and they were like a swarm of bees attacking to defend their queen.

Who the hell do they think they are?

They think they can just do as they please? It won't be long. We'll show them. I'll show them how to kneel properly.

The king—their dead king—had been right.

These females just need a very firm hand to teach them how to behave. To understand what their purpose is. They've been wayward long enough. Their islands were no longer a secret.

Not now that Clive and Merwin finally knew their location, thanks to their countless hours and days of patrolling with their former scout leader Stenlen.

Stenlen. Traitor.

The betrayal was a punch to his gut. Not just a betrayal to their king, but to Clive and Merwin too. They were a scout squad. The three of them. They'd been together for years. Decades.

The king's most loyal man, turned on him.

And for what? To *protect* those two females? It didn't make any sense. They'd spent all that time searching them out to bring them to heel. So what if Clive put a knife to one's throat? So what if the king threatened to impale his long-time prisoner? It was his right. His *right*!

He huffed.

The scent of land made the air dense. He adjusted his course to follow it. Merwin did likewise.

Back to their cache. To find a place to sleep and eat, and maybe something to screw to shake the knots out of his body. He didn't like being angry. It made him all tense and uncomfortable.

He frowned at the thought, which made his face hurt again. With his good eye, he glanced Merwin's way once again, noting the shredded flaps in his wings and the missing scales on his neck and shoulders. A broken spike made a gap in his crest.

Clive growled, turning his attention back toward the now-visible land mass.

They needed more guys.

More than that.

They needed to rebuild what the king's 'heir' had taken from them all.

Their home. Their way of life.

The king's efforts wouldn't be wasted. Clive would see to it. Maybe he could even take his place. Become the next real king, since the heir proved to be... disappointing.

Jori Mountainside. What kind of punk name is that? He'd rejected his blood name—his king's name. Kargassa. Richmund Kargassa, their murdered king.

Anger roiled through Clive's gut again.

The usurper, little better than the females, had been uninitiated.

Clive snorted as he angled his wings, preparing to land.

I'm going to honor my king. Take his name and keep his philosophy—*our* philosophies—our traditions alive.

And seek justice, one way or another.

Rebuild the tribe that Mountainside was destroying, take the females and their little islands, then regain control of the mountain lair.

His shifted to his human form as his feet touched land, heading toward their cache of clothes and supplies.

"Come on, we've got work to do."

"What work?"

"Recruiting."

Merwin shrugged. "Okay with me. Where to first?"

Clive considered the question as he pulled his clothes on. "Work our way up to Black River. They've got the best paranormal network to get the word out. And, they have a dragon refugee camp. I'm sure there'll be guys there that'll follow us and—what?"

He stepped back from Merwin peering at his face.

"You might want to get that looked at. Looks nasty."

Clive put a hand to his face, making himself wince. "Whatever. Let's just go."

Chapter 3

KOLINA HELPED THE SHIP'S captain moor the boat at the dock, exchanged some words of thanks, and made her way inland.

How long had it been since she last left the island?

Probably far too long.

But not so long she couldn't remember where Black River was.

Gingerly adjusting the mountaineering pack on her back, careful of her sore shoulder, she started walking.

About an hour after crossing out of the far side of the coastal town, a delivery truck slowed alongside her. A cloud of diesel assaulted her nose.

"Need a ride?" A woman's voice called through the open passenger side window.

Kolina glanced up to see the driver was alone in the cab of the truck and smiled. "Yes, thanks." As soon as the truck was fully stopped, she wasted no time unslinging her pack to climb in.

"Where ya headed?" The round-faced blonde asked.

"Black River."

"Oh, that's a ways, but you're in luck. It's on my route."

"I appreciate it."

"And I appreciate any conversation ya have. My favorite podcast hasn't updated yet and the radio stations around here suck. I'm Sarah," she said, checking her mirrors before easing the truck back into gear.

Kolina shrugged. "Kolina. I haven't got much conversation to share, but I'll do my best."

Sarah gave Kolina a side long glance. "Let me guess. Former military. Searching for something important, but don't know what or where yet?"

Kolina laughed. "Something like that. Meeting up with an old friend who might know where my daughter is. I'm going to be a grandmother."

The truck made it up to speed, engine groaning, bouncing them along the highway.

Sarah turned to Kolina with a full smile. "You're going to love it. Being a grandmother. All the fun without the responsibility." She winked and turned her attention back to the road.

Kolina liked Sarah's open and honest expression. She reminded her of the fisherwomen and craftswomen in the village. A breath of fresh sea air away from the constricted political atmosphere in the citadel.

She quickly learned that Sarah had four children of her own and five grandchildren. Divorced twice with a boyfriend waiting the other side of Black River for her.

"Have you been out to Black River before?"

"Years and years ago."

"Great little town. Has everything you'd need."

"Tell me about this podcast you mentioned." Kolina prompted.

Sarah drew a deep breath in excitement. "It's a paranormal podcast that started out as a radio show, more than a decade ago. They talk about everything you can think of. My favorite shows are the ones about the cryptids—and ghosts. I love me some ghost hunters."

"Cryptids?"

And on she went. Kolina tasted her excitement, prompting with more well-placed questions here and there. "Do you believe in all of it?"

Sarah shrugged her rounded shoulders. "Oh, I don't know. I've never seen any of it for myself. But why not? Wouldn't the world be a much more interesting place if that stuff was real?" She reached for her coffee flask and sipped. "Take your Black River, for example. There's all kinds of rumors about the place. Some folks think the Brandt family is a pack of werewolves and that the town is a paranormal hub!"

"Huh." Kolina supplied.

"Yeah! And just a few weeks ago the forums went wild with talk of dragon-people in town! The imagination of some people!"

"Really? What did they say about these... 'dragon-people'? And how would anyone know? Wouldn't they be hidden?"

"I know, right?" Sarah rolled her eyes. "There's some crazy guy that lives in town and runs this forum. He's convinced that every paranormal creature anyone can imagine has been through Black River at some point. I mean, really, it's just a quaint little town with 'Mom and Pop' shops."

"If these paranormals were real, wouldn't they have shut this forum down?"

"Seriously. That would make sense." Sarah blew out her breath with a chuckle. "Makes great reading though. When you spend as much time as I do on the roads, breaks up the monotony of dining alone. I can just scroll through the comments on my phone while I grab a sandwich and a coffee."

"Do *you* ever *see* anything?"

Sarah laughed then. A hearty 'Ha!' "Only when I've been driving too long. It's a great big flag to pull over and rest."

Kolina chuckled. "So what kind of flags do you get?"

Sarah frowned. "You know, come to think of it, right around the time the dragon-people posts exploded the forums, I thought I saw something big flying through the air. Several somethings big. But it was getting dark. And the lighting can play all kinds of tricks on your eyes when you're tired."

"No doubt." Kolina glanced across the landscape rolling toward them. It was nearing dusk.

Sarah flicked her headlights on as though she too just noticed the sun descending toward the undulating treetops that lined the growing mountain range. "Almost there."

Minutes stretched in bouncing silence.

The truck's headlights flashed across the wood carved sign heralding they'd reached the town boundary of Black River.

"I can let you off in the center of town."

"That's perfect. I appreciate the ride and conversation, Sarah."

Sarah smiled, still watching the road. "I rarely pick up hitchhikers. I just got a feeling." She glanced at Kolina. "Folks don't hitchhike as much as they used to. It generally isn't safe." Her tone turned heavy with sincere concern. "I mean, you look like you can probably take care of yourself, but still, be careful."

"I will. Don't worry about me."

"Maybe I'll catch you on your way back to the coast." Sarah's expression cleared, her smile returning. She found a gap among parked cars and pulled the truck over to the side of the main street.

Kolina grabbed her bag, opened the door and dropped to the sidewalk, then turned back to Sarah. "Maybe. Thanks again for the ride, Sarah. Drive safe."

Sarah gave her a little wave before Kolina swung the door closed and backed away from the truck. It expelled a little cloud of diesel as Sarah pulled away from the road and resumed her route.

Kolina looked up and down the street as she hauled her pack onto her back with a grunt. Pain shot through her wounded shoulder.

Streetlamps flickered to life. Most of the buildings were as she remembered them to be. But some of the shops were different from her last visit.

First stop; Blaine Brandt's bar, Soulfire, where Odson Blackridge worked.

"YEAH? SCREW YOU! ALL of you losers!" Clive screamed as he and his wing buddy Merwin walked down the dirt road away from the dragon refugee camp.

Several of the camp denizens watched them go, arms crossed over their chests, faces set in fierce scowls.

"They just don't get it, Clive. We don't want their sort in our tribe anyway," Merwin grumbled. "At least they fixed your face... mostly."

Clive sent him a scathing glare. From his good eye. "Shut up, Merwin. My face is fine."

"Hey, it ain't my fault they're all spineless and dimwitted. No need to be rude to me. Besides, it wasn't a complete loss. We got some of the younglings on board. Maybe that's the key, Clive. Find them young, before their little minds are tainted with ridiculous ideas of common dragon equality. There ain't no such thing."

Clive's glare turned to one of pained patience. "Yeah, sure, Merwin. A tribe of gangly younglings to take back the island."

"They'll grow."

"Yep. In a couple of decades, a few of them might even be big enough to throw at the females. We need mature males, Merwin. Not a bunch of kids."

"Patience. The king was a patient man. He spent many, many years building the mountain tribe up to what it was. We can do the same."

"I don't want to wait years." Clive snarled. "I want that island, and I want them to pay for what they did. Now!"

He ignored Merwin's assessing expression. "So do I, Clive. But we have to be smart about it. I think we should head south. One of the guys at the paranormal bar said there was a small tribe that might be interested in working with us."

Clive eyed the sun. Still a few hours before nightfall when they could take to the skies unseen. "Sure, why not? South it is."

Merwin pulled a phone from his pocket, thumbs tapping across the screen.

"What are you doing?"

"One of the younglings set up a forum. I'm just letting them know where we're headed in case they want to join us."

"Forum?"

"Yeah, to keep in touch. They can use it to get the word out and recruit more males of like mind."

"Huh. Smart."

"Got the idea from the local paranormal forum. Hiding in plain sight. Humans think it's all made up conspiracy stuff. But it's a public way to get news out."

Clive nodded, leaning in close to see what Merwin was typing on the phone.

"Looks pretty active already."

"It is. This is how we're going to grow. The young ones are useful at things like this."

Hope filled Clive as his anger fizzled away.

This could work.

Refugee camp forgotten, he grinned as they began walking south.

Chapter 4

KOLINA PULLED THE DOOR to the paranormal bar open and stepped inside. It was still an hour till it was officially open, so it was as quiet as she expected it to be.

A handsome young man looked up from piles of papers spread across the bar lining one side of the room. "We're not open yet, come back in an hour."

"Hello, Blaine. I haven't seen you since you were a cub." Kolina's lips stretched into a smile.

"Kolina Steelscale? Holy shit!" Blaine grinned back. "How the hell are you? You look exactly as I remember you. Does Mom know you're here? You're coming up to the house, right?"

"I'm looking for Odson. But yes, I have a gift to pass along to your mother."

Blaine's eyes twinkled. "I'm going to get bonus points for being the one to bring you in. Don't move, I'm just going to get my employee to take over for me."

Kolina laughed, enjoying his open humor.

A moment later, he reappeared, pulling on a jacket, a set of keys in his hand. "Let's go."

Retrieving her pack, she followed him out.

They chatted amiably on the drive up to the Brandt house. A lot had happened over the years. The Brandt cubs were all grown up now.

"By the way, you have a spy in town reporting on community events."

Blaine's eyes twinkled when he glanced at her with a grin.

She laughed. "But you know that already."

"Great way to get news out, while creating a screen of 'crazy' to the rest of the world."

She pulled a face. "As long as it doesn't backfire and attract trouble."

"Talking about a celebrity vlogger that fell from the sky and crashed into your island?"

"That would be who I'm thinking of, yes."

"Nice guy. Got a world of unexpected trouble on his plate right about now." He shot her another glanced. "That's why you're here."

"It is." She sighed, reminded of Jori Mountainside and Kymri again.

Blaine eased off the gas and turned onto a narrow road. Soon, the tree-lined road opened to expose the Brandt family home sprawling before them.

By the time Blaine parked the car and they got out of it, Heidi Brandt appeared at the screen door, wiping her hands on a dishtowel.

Kolina studied her old friend as she pulled her pack from the car and slung it over her good shoulder.

Heidi opened the door with a smile that lit her face, making Kolina feel as welcome as any Brandt family member.

Blaine breezed past his mother, swiping her cheek with is lips on his way to the door. "Did I miss dinner?" He disappeared inside.

"Kolina Steelscale. It's about time you brought your thick, scaly hide to see us."

"The queen sends her love."

Heidi's eyes narrowed. "In the form of a bottle of Aeleftherian wine?"

"Isn't it always?" She laughed, climbing the porch steps. She stopped and they stood eye to twinkling eye, studying the minute differences in each other's face. "She wants you to visit."

Heidi pulled Kolina into a hug and scoffed. "When do I have time to visit a beautiful, hidden tropical island in the middle of nowhere? Family keeps me busy. This community keeps me busy." She laughed as she pulled away to open the screen door, sweeping a hand for Kolina to precede her inside.

The distinct scent of black bear—*Brandt family* bear—enveloped Kolina with its familiarity. She'd almost forgotten its particular essence of deep forest and wild ursine.

Her eyes swept the picture-filled walls. So many more smiling faces since her last visit.

Heidi led her straight toward the kitchen, turned, and held out her hand.

Kolina grinned as she carefully unslung her pack, unzipped one of the many compartments and extracted the perfectly aged Queens' blend of Aeleftherian berries.

Heidi admired the hand-crafted bottle, which Kolina knew had been blown by one of the island artisans that lived on the west side of the island.

"How long are you staying?" Heidi asked, setting the bottle on the counter island to retrieve wine glasses from the cupboard and a corkscrew from a drawer.

Kolina shrugged. "Not long. I'm here on business."

"Of course you are. When aren't you?" Heidi pinned her with her gaze and a smirk as she worked the cork out of the bottle. "You're chasing the trouble your daughter and her young man stirred up."

"I'm always chasing trouble. That's what I do."

"The Aeleftheria way. We don't see tooth nor claw of you Aeleftherians for years at a time—decades even, then all of a sudden, dragons everywhere descending on our little town getting everyone's hackles raised."

It was Kolina's turn to snort as she accepted the glass. "You always make it sound as though we're all drama."

Heidi raised a brow then turned her attention to the sapphire blue liquid swirling in her own glass. "Thank Her Majesty for me."

"Thank her yourself when you visit her." Kolina pushed.

Heidi sipped, savored, and swallowed with a sigh. "This is going on the top shelf where the boys know better than to touch it. Are you hungry? We just finished dinner, but there are leftovers."

Kolina shook her head. "Where is everyone?"

Heidi led Kolina to the living room, where plush sofas were angled for conversation and optimal fireplace enjoyment. "Dispersed as soon as their bellies were full. They'll be back tomorrow."

They curled up to chat as though there were catching up after a week's break rather than years.

That's how it was with Heidi. She made everyone welcome to her home as though it were theirs to relax. One of the very few places Kolina allowed herself to let her role as Queen's Guardian peel away. "It's good to see you again, old friend."

"And you too. How is Launia?"

"Overseeing all of the island guardian fleets."

"So, in a constant state of stress then."

"More or less. It seems we all are, for a long time now."

Heidi's expression turned serious. "I met Kymri. Oh, she reminded me so very much of you. Fierce and stubborn."

Kolina studied the flames from the fireplace, reflected in the blue wine.

"Congratulations, and welcome to the grandmothers club."

"Ha!" Kolina exploded. "I never thought I would be excited to step into that role. But as soon as the shamans told me she had a youngling in her belly... I don't know. Something within me changed. Changed in a different way from when I was with child."

Heidi nodded. "It is different."

Kolina chuckled. "Kymri thought I had lost my mind when we learned of her pregnancy."

"We do, you know. Lose our minds when grandchildren come about."

The lightness that had begun to weave its way around Kolina dimmed. "You're aware of what happened when she left here?"

"Odson told me what he knew, which wasn't much. The king had his henchmen looking for Kymri's young man. Apparently Jori was his heir."

Kolina sucked in a breath, her heart began pounding in her ears. She could see the queen's explosive reaction in her mind's eye. This just became so much more complicated.

The king's heir.

What the dragons' hell had happened?

Is Kymri in danger?

"You didn't know?" Heidi's brows rose.

"Marli failed to include *that* in her report." She drew a deep breath, considering what little there was in the transcripts. "They came here to see you, then went to Blaine's club to meet with Odson's friends for help. They were separated when Kymri and Jori Mountainside disappeared. Then, her report just said that Jori called Odson from the mountain lair and said that the king was dead, they were safe, and Elora was with them."

"She is still alive? That must have been an incredible reunion between her and Jori. I can't imagine being separated from any of my boys for so long like that." Heidi's voice dropped with the depth of her empathy. She searched Kolina's eyes. "You must be worried about Kymri, pregnant and in the king's lair like that."

Kolina set her nearly empty glass on the coffee table. "I should find Odson. I need him to tell me where the lair is. I have to find Kymri and Elora."

"He's there—at the lair. He and Jori's human father, Jonathan, flew out there together. Odson stopped here to tell us he'd be away for a little while so that Blaine could find someone to cover his shifts, but he didn't say much about the whole affair."

Kolina laughed, in a brittle way. "It's a good thing the king is already dead, if Odson went there. Otherwise, Odson would have done it himself. When did he go?"

"As soon as Jori called him... so a few weeks at least. He's due back any time now." Heidi turned thoughtful for a moment. "Odson is a good man. I know how the queen feels about having males anywhere near the island, but..." her voice trailed away.

"You think she should reunite the tribes."

"What do *you* think?" Heidi challenged Kolina.

"I'm loyal. I follow my queen's decisions."

"You've never challenged her?"

Kolina picked up the glass and tipped the last of the liquor down her throat. Her free hand rubbed the locket hidden under her shirt, pressed to her breastbone.

"The Council doesn't leave room for mind-changing. She's always known what was at stake. Ultimately the decisions are hers, but they put an incredible amount of pressure on her."

Heidi's voice softened. "As I said, I couldn't imagine being separated from my boys. I've watched Odson over the years. He keeps his distance from everyone."

"Don't say it. I know. I know that the separation of the sexes has caused extremist views on both sides. I see it. But with the recent attack, there's no way we can let our guard down, even though the king is dead. If Jori doesn't just resume what he started, someone else probably will."

Heidi shrugged. "Maybe things will change with him in the mountain? He didn't strike me as the dominant male type when I met him."

"No, I didn't think so either. But he hadn't been initiated. And as for the attacks, that's why I'm here; there's been another. Our guardians recognized two of the same dragons that attacked us before." She gestured to her lame arm. "I have to find out what's going on; how the king died and what kind of threat level we're facing now. When there's a new king on the throne, any sense of stability gets shaken up."

Heidi nodded. She understood. "I don't know how long before Odson comes back, so I guess you're just stuck here with us."

"I do need to get there as soon as possible, but I could think of worse ways to bide my time. May as well put me to work while I'm here." Kolina's lips quirked at the corner.

Heidi grinned. "You bet I will." She swallowed the last of the blue wine in her glass. "Now, tell me everything that's happened on that island of yours since the last time you were here."

Chapter 5

SEVERAL DAYS PASSED WITH Kolina spending all her time in Heidi's domestic domain. She was sure she'd met every member of the Brandt family by the end of the second day. Blaine got the word out and everyone came by at one point or another to meet her.

The tone of life here was so much different than home.

The Brandts still had their problems, as everyone did. Shifter politics. No one could escape it.

But what was different was the sense of balance between the sexes that Aeleftheria lacked.

Kolina stood vigil while some of Heidi's grand-cubs romped through the yard, while their parents disappeared for 'adult' time.

She couldn't help remembering Kymri at that age.

Everything about this visit to Black River was bittersweet. Despite the situation, the solid family atmosphere ripped the past out of its place in her psyche and shoved it in her face to re-examine.

Her dragon's voice was soft when she spoke to her, sharing her buried heart ache.

We made our choices.

I know.

"Kolina, are you alright?" Heidi approached with a steaming mug of Gen-Mai tea.

Kolina blinked, forcing a semblance of a smile to her lips. "Thank you. Yes, I'm fine."

Heidi's gaze slide from Kolina's face to her grand-children playing nearby. "You're worried about Kymri? She'll be safe with him—Jori I mean. I had a good sense of him when they were here."

Kolina turned to assess Heidi's sincerity.

Positive outlook or *knowing* something more?

The look in Heidi's eyes told her it was something more.

"Thank you for that." She sucked in a breath. "I was thinking about Kymri...and about my son." She nodded toward the children, allowing the pent-up tension to ease from her shoulders. As she did so, the left one tinged, making her wince.

"Not quite healed yet?" Heidi watched Kolina closely.

Kolina rubbed at her shoulder with her free hand. "Almost. It's probably good that I'm here and not back home. Forces me to be on my best behavior. I'm a terrible patient."

"Odson called while I was in the house. He'll be back in Black River sometime tonight and out to the house in the morning."

"You told him I was here?"

Heidi nodded, her eyes lingering on Kolina's face.

"What is it?" she asked, becoming suspicious.

Her old friend shrugged, sipping her tea. "I may have suggested he take you with him to deliver some things for me when you leave."

"Where to?"

"You'll see." She turned to the prowling children. "Cookie time!"

Several sets of ears perked, noses twitched, then furry bodies clamored over each other, racing for the steps to the house, turning to naked little human forms, chubby hands reaching for the door handle in an effort to be the first to the fresh baked treats.

ODSON HAD ARRIVED.

The distinct growl of a muscle car grew louder as it approached the property, then cut just outside the house.

Kolina and Heidi glanced at one another from across the dining room table, set their cups aside and made their way to the front door.

Heavy boots clunked up the wooden steps two at a time.

Heidi opened the front inner door as the screen door opened to reveal Odson Blackridge.

"Good morning," he growled, in his Odson way.

"Coffee?" Heidi offered. "You look like you flew all night."

He shook his head. "No thanks. And I did." Turning his shuttered gaze to Kolina, he said, "ready to go?"

"Of course," she replied, falling back into her formal Aeleftherian role. She picked up her pack from beside the front door, sliding her arms into the straps, and picked up a box, ignoring the strain on her shoulder.

Heidi had half a dozen boxes stacked beside the door that Odson was meant to deliver for her. They quickly moved them to his trunk and backseat.

Kolina placed her pack in the car then went to hug Heidi. "You're going to visit Aeleftheria if I have to fly you there myself," she threatened.

"Promise?" Heidi laughed, squeezing her tight.

They said their good-byes and Kolina got into Odson's Mustang Shelby.

He exchanged a few words with Heidi before getting in behind the wheel, then started the car and turned it toward the main road.

They hadn't seen each other since Odson and Marli had left the island with Kymri and Jori to try to find the male tribe's lair.

No one had reported its location to the queen and her council.

Kolina opened her mouth to speak.

Odson cut her off, "Kymri and the baby are fine."

It wasn't what she was going to ask but hearing those words of assurance eased the tension in her gut. Her breath slid out and the next she drew was long and deep, steadying the unexpected surge of relief.

She nodded. "I'll bring her and Elora home to the queen."

Odson snorted. "Good luck with that." He turned the car onto the main road and hit the gas, jolting them forward.

Kolina narrowed her eyes on his profile. "You'll tell me where they are."

He shrugged. "If they want me to, I will."

"Why wouldn't they?" Surprise thumped her chest.

He didn't answer.

He didn't have to.

She already knew the answer.

Why wouldn't they?

Because things had changed and they no longer wished to live under the queen's rule?

Kolina swallowed, worry ignited her pulse, making her heart thump.

But Odson had just said they were fine.

She straightened her shoulders. "There was another attack on the island. Two of the three males that attacked before."

Odson grunted.

"Marli didn't report that Jori was the king's heir."

His lips compressed.

"Heidi told me."

"I told you, Kymri and the baby are fine. We're not *all* domineering asshats, Kolina."

"Are you going to make those assurances to the queen?"

"I only go to the island when I absolutely have to. And at this point in time, I don't have to."

Kolina ground her teeth.

She studied Odson's profile again. Now that they were confined to the close space of the car with little else to look at than passing road and trees, she paid closer attention to the signals in his visage.

At their last meeting, in the queen's chamber, where he and Jori had revealed their stories of Elora's disappearances—not one, but two disappearances—Jori had held most of Kolina's focus.

She didn't know of any other species that aged slower than dragons, other than maybe the Djinn. So it wasn't that Odson looked 'older'. No, he looked exhausted.

Which would account for his terse rudeness.

Terse was generally a good description of Odson, but not usually rude.

He seemed resolved not to tell her anything useful, so she remained silent until they turned off the main highway and down another gravel road with 'No Exit' and 'No Trespassing' signs posted to either side several feet behind a deep ditch lined with thick pines.

Arriving at a sturdy gate barring the road, Odson parked the car, but left it running as he got out and punched a covered keypad with his index finger. He returned to the driver's seat as the gate slid open. They passed through and Kolina saw the gate slide closed through her side-view mirror.

Wherever they were going, visitors weren't welcomed with open arms.

They drove down the lane, a plume of gravel dust extending behind them.

Arriving at another set of posts, this time the second gate was already open, and manned.

Odson slowed to a stop, rolling his window down to speak to the woman dressed in jeans and an open plaid shirt over a faded tee. "Hey Odson, welcome back."

"Heidi Brandt sent us."

Leaning on the open window of Odson's door, the woman bent to peer into the back of the car, then to Kolina. Her gaze narrowed on Kolina's chest.

Kolina glanced down. Her locket rested on the outside of her shirt; the queen's winged-shield insignia caught the sunlight.

"What the hell is *she* doing here?" Her voice, no longer the friendly tone that welcomed Odson, had turned accusatory and hard. "She can't be here."

"She's helping me with the boxes from Heidi Brandt's place."

"We don't need help. Especially not from her. We can unload the boxes here and bring them to the center later. Thank Mrs. Brandt for us."

Odson's hand flashed out, catching the woman's as she straightened to back away. "She's a Brandt family guest."

The woman bent again, brows furrowed, scowling at Kolina.

To Odson she said, "you know I'd do anything for Heidi Brandt, but having her here is asking a lot."

"I know it. She knows it too. She always has a reason."

"Which is?"

Odson shrugged.

"She better not cause any shit while she's here, Odson. You're responsible for her." She stepped away from the car.

Odson sighed and gave her a curt nod.

"What's going on? What is this place?" Kolina kept her voice low, gaze swinging across the windshield.

Make-shift huts and timber houses, interspersed with tents, made up a small village.

The second gate slid closed behind them.

"This is the dragon refugee camp."

"Refugee camp? Refugees from what?"

Odson spared her a pained glance, before pulling up in front of a building that was more solid than most of the others. "The queen. Other tribes. Anyone what doesn't want to be told how to live." He got out of the car and popped the trunk.

More locals approached. Kolina got out to help unload the boxes from Heidi.

"Why didn't I know about it?"

"Why would you need to?"

She was getting tired of his attitude. But she needed him to tell her how to find the mountain lair where Kymri and Elora were.

She held her tongue as she passed a box to a young man.

Her nostrils flared, catching scents from around what appeared to a community center. Almost all dragons. Almost, but not quite. A few humans, a few other shifters and one or two scents she couldn't name.

Another, familiar face appeared in the doorway, locking eyes with her.

"Fiona?"

One of younger female dragons from the town on Aeleftheria.

"Honor Guardian Steelscale." She stiffened, eyes darting between Kolina and the car.

The young man that had taken the box from Kolina moved to take Fiona's hand, standing protectively in front of her. Fiona moved out from behind him and strode toward Kolina.

"You can tell them I'm not going back," she said.

Kolina's brows rose. "Does your mother know?"

Fiona stiffened and sniffed. "She'd just tell me it was my duty to go back."

Before Kolina could stop herself, she said, "She's right. It's the duty of all of us to protect our culture and follow our traditions. To obey our queen."

The young man growled.

Odson glared at Kolina.

"Your queen. Not mine!" Fiona shouted, color rising in her pale face.

"It's okay Fiona, I won't let her take you from us. Just don't get upset." He placed a protective hand over her abdomen.

Kolina blinked, noticing now that her belly was rounded.

"You're bonded?"

"No," The young man said, "but we don't need to be. We chose to be together."

Kolina's eyes flicked back to Fiona. "Your choice? Not forced?"

Fiona shook her head. "My choice."

Kolina noted Odson's attention flicking around them.

She turned, noting the crowd that grew around the car. Most of the faces staring at her were hostile. Some just curious.

Fuck.

Heidi had wanted her to see a community of dragons living together—a balance of male and female.

"Come on." Odson closed the trunk with a *thunk* and led Kolina inside the community center. "I'll introduce you to the refugee's council."

Oh, this ought to be interesting.

Chapter 6

THE BOXES HAD BEEN set on a series of tables pushed to one side of the room where piles of folded clothing and household supplies were piled.

Odson introduced Kolina to a dragoness called Brandi.

Brandi's gaze slid from Odson to Kolina. "Look, we don't want any trouble here. We've already sent away a couple of guys trying to stir things up."

Odson frowned. "What happened?"

"Don't worry about it. We get them now and then. Think they can come here and turn things around like we're all desperate for a savior of some kind."

"Male dragons? What do you know about them?" Kolina asked. "They could be from the king's mountain."

"Oh, they were." Brandi said. "They had a lot to say about that. Seems they were kicked out. Some usurper. We don't care about whatever power squabbles are going on over there, until they come spilling into our camp. We patched them up, let them stay a few days then strongly suggested they be on their way when they started with their bullshit."

"Patched them up?"

"Bullshit?"

Kolina and Odson prompted at once.

"Yeah, seemed they'd gotten into some kind of scuffle and dragged their sorry tails here. No surprise either. They wouldn't shut up about male dragon rights. They were too stupid to realize they were in the wrong camp for that crap." She pinned her gaze to Kolina. "We live here together, as equals. That won't change."

"Could be the same two that attacked us." Kolina said.

Odson nodded. "Probably. Clive and Merwin. They've been to Black River before. To take Jori to the king. Sounds like they came here to lick their wounds."

"Sounds like they came here seeking sympathetic minds." Brandi snorted. "And yeah, those are their names. Not the brightest, but certainly dangerous. When they realized none of our men were interested in their Kool-Aid, they started striking up conversations with some of the younger guys and boys. That's when we sent them on their way."

"Sounds like they're trying to keep the old king's vision alive."

"They were very loyal to him. It's no wonder they're bitter about Jori stepping into Richmund's position as king. He's the complete opposite of his sire."

"Jori Mountainside is the new king?" Kolina sputtered, heart pounding. "What the hell happened? When he left the island with you and Kymri, he was human—uninitiated."

"Long story short? The king tried to initiate him, but he hadn't accounted for the binding spell Elora had put on Jori's dragon magic, or the sense of righteousness in his psyche. They didn't tell me much about what happened. Just that the king threatened Elora and Kymri's lives if he didn't comply. The king lost his. Now Jori's got a male tribe to figure out how to lead and reprogram."

"Reprogram?"

"He's not down with the way things have been run." Odson turned to Brandi. "He's trying to turn things the way you did here. Find balance between the dragon sexes."

"Huh." Brandi said.

"He won't be able to do it. How many others, aside from the two that attacked us, have gone rogue?"

"Well, they're going to be limited as to where they can go. Most other dragon colonies don't operate with a division of the sexes like you do on your island. It's archaic."

"We did what we had to." Kolina snapped. "We wouldn't have survived otherwise."

"And so you did. And now things are changing."

"Are they?" Kolina snarled. "Just because this young, inexperienced, *new* dragon sauntered into the king's mountain, doesn't mean he can change centuries of ingrained bias overnight. Those two males attacked our island just weeks ago, intent on destroying the most vulnerable citizens. That doesn't fucking sound like change to me."

"Kolina." Odson cut in. "They were two of many. Only two. And Richmund is dead. No longer an influential force over that tribe. Jori is already changing things."

"Until they figure out a way to kill him, I'll wager. It isn't the dragon way to follow the weak."

"No, it isn't." Odson said, straightening. "He's inexperienced, but he isn't weak. You don't know him."

"He's one dragon in a lair of how many?"

"He isn't alone. He very quickly formed a council, headed by Elora, Kymri, Stenlen and several others loyal to the kingship."

"Isn't Stenlen one of the three that attacked us the first time?"

Odson shrugged. "One of the king's strongest men. He's loyal to the crown and doesn't believe in harming females. So, you may as well just go back to Queen Regina and tell her things are under control."

"This is wild." Brandi said.

Kolina's gaze narrowed on Brandi. "Thought you didn't care what happened in the mountain?"

"Dragon drama at its best."

Kolina rolled her eyes and turned her focus back to Odson. "And no, it's not under control. There are at least two male dragons out there that tried to destroy one of the villages below the citadel. How many more next time? Thanks to Jori, we're no longer hidden. Our queen is no longer safe."

"You all knew it was just a matter of time and—"

"We did. And the time came when we had to defend ourselves from male attacks. Again. Richmund tried to find us for as long as we've occupied that little archipelago."

"And now he's dead."

"His vision clearly isn't."

"It will die too. Eventually."

Kolina shook her head. "I don't believe that. And the longer Elora and Kymri are in that lair, the more danger they're in. I need to take them home."

"They won't go."

"We'll see about that."

They stared at each other for a long moment.

Brandi broke the silence. "Odson, please thank Heidi for the donations. It was very kind. You're both welcome to stay, as long as there is no ideological or political talk."

"That sounds rather repressive, doesn't it?"

"That's the rule for outsiders."

"The queen thanks you for your hospitality, but I do have to be going." She strode toward the door, stopped, and turned to Odson. "I'll get my pack from your car. If you'll tell me where the lair is, I'll be on my way."

Odson shook his head, said his good-byes to Brandi, then approached Kolina and said, "I'll take you there if I get word from Jori that you may go."

Kolina bristled, falling in step behind him as he continued out of the center toward his car.

Why wouldn't Jori want her to be there? What are they hiding?

Her eyes narrowed on Odson's broad back.

"What aren't you telling me, Odson?"

At the bottom of the steps, he spun around, brows raised. "Probably an awful lot that isn't your business, or the queen's business, until Jori decides it is."

Her own brows shot up as she stomped down the stairs to face him toe to toe, which wasn't easy given how much taller he was. "I demand you give me Kymri's location."

Odson chuckled.

Kolina's fingers curled into fists. She stared at him.

"Odson?" A woman's tentative voice broke their eye-lock as Odson spun to face whoever had called his name.

Kolina's eyes flicked toward a woman standing next to Odson's car, hands shoved in her pockets, shoulders hunched.

"What is it, Allison?" He moved toward her. "We'll discuss this later," he shot over his shoulder.

Kolina growled at his back. He ignored her.

She followed Odson toward his car. She needed her pack from it.

If he was going to screw around, she'd just have to figure out where the tribe's lair was on her own. She'd already wasted too much time here, no matter how much she'd enjoyed spending time with Heidi Brandt.

Her shoulder was nearly healed enough that she'd be able to fly. It would take time, but if she had to resort to nightly flight patrols to search for it, she would.

And no matter Odson's assurances that Kymri and Elora were safe, she didn't trust him. He'd withheld vital information before, there was no reason he wouldn't continue to do so.

Why would he hesitate to tell her where the lair was?

Maybe things weren't as he'd said they were.

Why wouldn't Jori enforce his newfound power and subdue the females in his new kingdom? It would be easy.

"... and it's not like him to just go off without a word." The woman's voice rose.

Kolina reined in her thoughts, catching the conversation between the woman and Odson. She opened the back door of the Shelby to retrieve her pack.

"What happened?" Odson asked, his voice grave.

"I don't know." The woman looked up into his concerned face. "He stopped telling me about what was going on in his life—that's why he was going to you. But something happened while you were gone. And those two guys were hanging around him and his friends. Did he say anything to you before you left?"

Odson shook his head. "He came to talk to me about a girl in the camp he'd been agonizing over for some time. I suggested he just talk to her and ask her out. Then he'd know one way or another. Maddy, I think her name is."

She nodded, then blew out a breath. "She's dating someone. A non-dragon shifter."

"He'll be disappointed. Probably just needs some time to process. I'm sure he'll be back." He placed a hand on her shoulder then pulled her into a hug.

Kolina had never seen this side of Odson before.

"What if he doesn't? We've been arguing a lot lately. He's been so edgy—angry."

"He's a good kid, he'll be back. Besides, he's a dragon, he can take care of himself." He pulled back and grinned down into her distraught face. "Just blowing off steam."

"I hope you're right. I just felt...unsettled with those two strangers lurking around the boys. Some of them left too. But this is the first time Ben has done it. And I don't want to be that overbearing mom invading his privacy." She bit her lip. "He's been so volatile lately. I don't want to push him away even more."

"I'll look into it." He squeezed her shoulder and managed a gentle smile before she turned away and left them without a word to Kolina.

Kolina couldn't believe it.

Odson Blackridge smiled.

Chapter 7

"COME ON. YOU'RE GOING to help me find this kid while we're waiting for Jori to get back to us. I'm your quickest way to that lair...if they grant you permission." Odson smirked.

And just like that, the sense of wonder over this new side of Odson dissipated with a crisp 'pop'.

Odson dragged Kolina back and forth across the camp looking for youth and supposed family members of the young dragon shifter.

"Why don't you just summon everyone?"

Odson snorted. "This isn't the island, Honor Guardian Steelscale. People here have lives, and work to do, and appreciate discretion."

"As do we," she snapped. "If the mother is so worried about the disappearance of her child, shouldn't she be looking for him herself? Why does she need *you*?"

He stopped walking and turned to face her, forcing her to stop short, lest she collide with him. "I thought you had more tact than this, Kolina. You've been shut away on that damned island for far too long. Aren't you supposed to be some politician in training or something by now?"

Kolina sniffed. "I am tactful when it's necessary. This is just some spoiled little hormonal male dragon that didn't get what he wanted, so he ran away."

Odson shrugged. "Probably. Or he's a heartbroken little male dragon that's trying to figure out how to process his emotions without a dad around to teach him how."

"What is there to process? The female rejected him. He has to accept it and move on."

"Is that what you teach all the females on Aeleftheria?"

Had she detected derision? Was he snarling at her?

"That's how Steelscales are taught to manage their emotions. There are more important things to focus on."

"Like the queen's wellbeing."

"And that of her citizens living on the island. There's little time to run away and feel sorry for ourselves when we have to spend all our time training so we can defend ourselves. Sometimes to the death, because we won't allow some fragile males to take us away to satisfy their poor little egos."

Odson's voice dropped, his expression turned pitiable as he regarded her. "Not everyone lives like that, Kolina. Nor do *you* have to."

She gaped at him. "You did hear me when I said the island was attacked? Again. Why is it so hard for that to get through your thick skull, Odson? You know us. You know why we live in segregation. You know why we have to protect ourselves."

"How long will you all keep living like that?"

Kolina ground her teeth. There was no reasoning with him. She shook her head.

The tension across her shoulders and through her belly knotted tighter.

I thought he understood us. I guess I was wrong. We all were.

Males.

She huffed, trying to suppress her mistrust. Her free hand sought the locket under her shirt, pulling it free, then slid it back and forth along its chain. A growing habit to curb her mounting frustration. Pressing it to her lips, thoughtful, she sighed and let it drop to dangle free.

Compassion. How would she have handled such a situation?

Given the mistakes she'd made with Kymri, she couldn't be so quick to judge.

"Where to now?" she changed the subject.

"Town."

She turned and strode back toward where they'd left the car.

ᵠᵠᵠ

IT WAS LATE AFTERNOON by the time Odson rolled the Shelby to a stop across from Blaine Brandt's bar, slid it into park and put the engine to sleep. Kolina shot Odson a glance before scanning the rest of the street. There were a few pedestrians going about their business.

Odson strode across the street toward the bar; Kolina followed. He didn't go in the front door but led her around the corner to the alley, where he unlocked a steel door and motioned for her to precede him.

She cast him a quick glance, but he was stone-faced, closed off to her again.

Shoving aside the stab of regret, she stepped into the building.

He closed the outer door then led the way to a crowded office where they found Blaine Brandt.

"Hey Odson, welcome back. Kolina, I thought you left this morning." He stood, eyes wide in surprise.

"Seems Odson is determined to keep me in Black River a little longer, and to have me make new friends at a dragon camp." She offered him a wan smile.

Blaine's brows rose as he turned to Odson. "My mother?"

Odson nodded.

Blaine chuckled and shrugged.

"I came by to ask about the youth—what've you heard?"

Blaine studied Odson a moment. "You look like you need a good night's sleep, Odson." He blew out a breath and rubbed a hand over his face. "While you were gone, some of the younger male dragons have been getting into typical mischief. Nothing serious. At least not until a couple of adult males showed up. The males that were here the night your friend disappeared."

Odson nodded. "I know who you mean. So, they were here all the time I was gone?"

Blaine shook his head. "From what I've heard they came and went. Then one night, they came back all beat up and looking worse for wear. More aggressive than before. Talking to the younger males. There's been chatter that they're putting ideas in their heads. The paranormal community is on edge, Odson. No one wants dragon problems in their town."

"I know, I know. Keep the peace. I'll do what I can." Odson promised. "What else can you tell me?"

"Some of the youth came to town, pushing their way around. Picking fights. Thankfully they had enough sense to stay in human form."

"Here?"

Blaine nodded. "Outside. A couple were arrested for disturbing the peace after I told them to leave."

"Shit. What about those other two guys?"

Blaine shrugged again. "I haven't seen them around in a few days."

"Those are the same two that attacked Aeleftheria." Kolina said.

"If I'd known—"

"I know."

"Thanks, Blaine. I'll get this straightened out."

"Do you know where they went?"

"The adults? Nah. But if I hear anything more, I'll give you a heads up, now that I know they're the same guys."

"You should have let me know what was going on while I was gone." Odson said.

"Odson." Blaine said, letting his voice drop.

Odson blew out a breath. "Yeah, I know, sorry. You're not my secretary."

"And you're not actually responsible for all of the dragons in the area."

"I know."

"Though the population is getting dangerously high."

Odson scrubbed a hand over his tired face. "I know that, too. I'll let the camp council know there needs to be another meeting."

"Do you know what their long-term plans are?"

Odson shook his head. "Most of the time, I stay out everyone else's business."

"Looks to me like you're firmly entrenched in their business." Kolina said.

"I'm not. This is different." Odson glared at Kolina. He turned his focus back to Blaine. "Thanks, man."

Blaine nodded and said his good-byes to Kolina. "It was really good to see you again."

Kolina smiled. "Likewise."

Once they left the bar, Odson didn't go back to his car, but instead strode up the street.

"Where are we going now?" She demanded as she followed him.

"Police station." He grunted.

"You want me to report the two dragon males to the police?"

"You can if you want to." He shrugged. "I have other business."

"What other business?"

"Peace disturbers."

"This is a waste of my time. Just unlock your car so I can get my pack and I'll look for the lair myself."

"You won't find it. You'll just waste your time. Just wait for Jori to give the okay, and I'll take you there myself. Once this business with the kids is sorted out."

"I'd rather spend a few nights flying around searching for it, than waste my time running around this town with you chasing spoiled young dragon males."

"I'd rather you would too. But Heidi Brandt asked me to help you, and as a courtesy to the queen, I will. And no, I don't know why Jori hasn't answered yet, but I'm sure there's a good reason."

This did nothing to alleviate Kolina's concerns about the situation at the lair.

No one currently knew the location of the two males that attacked the island. They could be staging another attack now.

I'd rather be on the island preparing to defend it than wasting anymore time here.

"It's been hours, Odson."

"I know. We'll give it a few more."

She caught the flicker of concern in his eyes before he turned his face back in the direction they were walking.

Minutes later, they strode up the front steps to the heritage building that was Black River's Police Station and jail.

"They're all good kids, y'know," Odson grunted as he yanked the glass door open.

Kolina didn't answer as she followed him into the stone building.

She hung back as he spoke to an officer at the counter.

"Good kids that you're currently bailing out of jail," she said once the officer was busy making calls and Odson had returned to stand beside her.

"And youth on Aeleftheria never get into trouble?"

"Of course they do, but not often."

"And how is that handled?"

"We keep them busy with their duties. Give them something to focus on so they don't become lost and misguided."

"And those that still don't fall in line?"

She stared at him. "They usually choose to leave."

"And form camps, or wander tribeless."

"What's your point?" She snapped, already knowing what he was going to say. "That our system is causing more problems than it solves? You think we don't know there are flaws? No system is flawless, I—"

"Odson?"

Kolina and Odson turned to see a young man, mid to late teens, standing by the front desk, shoulders hunched. Another young man stood a step or two behind him, arms crossed, shoulder leaning against the wall, glaring at everyone in the room.

"Ben. Darren."

"My mom called you, didn't she?" The one that spoke moved forward.

"She's worried about you, Ben."

"She needs to mind her own damned business." The other, Darren growled. "We were fine."

Odson's brow rose. "Is that right?"

"Yeah." Darren said, pushing off of the wall and stepping forward to stand next to Ben. "We didn't need you to come and rescue us. Come on, Ben. Let's get out of here."

"Spoiled, entitled males," Kolina growled.

"Who the hell are you?" Darren spat. "Spoiled? Entitled? Screw you, bitch. You don't know us.

"No, she doesn't. But I do. If you're just fine, then you can pay back the bail money I just dropped for both of you."

"We don't have any money." Darren glared at Kolina.

"No one will hire us." Ben said.

"Dirty camp kids." Darren mimicked.

In that moment, Kolina saw the hurt fueling the youngling's anger.

"How many places did you try? Two?" Odson demanded.

Both younglings dropped their eyes to the floor.

Odson huffed. "Two? And now you're feeling sorry for yourselves and swinging fists, raging at the world. I bet you feel like somebody now that you've spent a couple of nights in jail."

Ben nudged at a scuff in the tiled floor with the toe of his shoe.

"He doesn't look so angry to me," Kolina said, nodding to Ben, then looked at Darren. "That one, though..."

"What business is it of yours?" Darren demanded.

"Come on, I'll drive you home," Odson said, heading for the door.

As Kolina moved to follow him out, she heard Darren mutter to Ben.

"I'm not going back. There's nothing for me there. You going back to your 'mommy'?"

"You've got your dad. Where are you going?"

Darren snorted. "He's so drunk all the time, he doesn't even know I exist. I'm going south to catch up to the others."

Kolina held the door open, waiting for the boys to exit the building.

Ben mumbled, "thanks."

Darren scowled his way past her, his eyes flicking to hers, then caught the insignia on the exposed locket. "You're one of *them*."

She met his gaze. The hurt and anger were replaced by cold hatred.

"Our friends will want to know about *her*." Darren said to Ben, jerking his head toward Kolina.

"What friends?" Odson demanded from the foot of the steps.

"*Friends*." Darren drew out the word like it was a foreign concept to Odson. "Nothing you know a damned thing about."

"He just got you out of jail," Kolina said.

"Yeah, so he can get into Ben's mom's pants."

"Hey!" Ben said.

"What? You're going to tell me you can't see how he sniffs after her and she strings him along?"

Ben's cheeks flushed red as his eyes narrowed on his friend. "Don't talk about her like that."

"Why, because she's your mom? She just a female like all the others. Playing coy, like she's got something special between her legs." To Odson he said, "man up and screw her. Get on with life already. That's what she's there for."

Ben's fist shot out toward Darren's mouth. Darren's head snapped back, making him stumble backward down several steps, surprise widening his eyes.

Darren lunged toward Ben, but Odson was already between them. Darren bounced off of Odson's outstretched hand, blocking his attack on his friend.

Ben struggled against Odson's other hand trying to reach Darren to hit him again.

Kolina crossed her arms, watching the scene. After another moment, she said "I'll meet you at your car." She strode past Odson and the snarling boys who had turned on each other like dogs fighting over a piece of marked territory.

Chapter 8

Kolina leaned against Odson's classic Shelby, legs crossed at the ankle, waiting.

I'll bet those friends the boy mentioned are the male dragons that attacked Aeleftheria.

What to do now?

Let Odson and the locals deal with the problems here and continue on her way to the mountain lair? Or pursue the offending males?

And do what?

She sighed.

Several guardian patrols had trouble defending the island against the two full grown males.

If I can find their base and assess their position and numbers, I might be able to forewarn the Council.

Or, I can continue my mission to assess the potential threat from the mountain lair, and get Kymri and Elora home.

Those two males were already a proven threat to her people, and it was only a matter of time before the next attack. The status of the mountain dragons at this time was unknown.

'I'm going south to catch up to the others,' the boy, Darren, had said.

Just the two males? Likely more.

Movement up the sidewalk drew her attention. Odson and the boy, Ben, were headed toward her and the car.

Odson had insisted that Jori was trustworthy.

But did she trust Odson's judgment?

He was one of the few males she had trusted in the past. It was only recent events surrounding Elora that had rattled that trust. She had to grudgingly admit it was a hard situation which she understood all too well, even if she disagreed with the final decision.

Odson unlocked the car without another word to Kolina.

She pulled her pack from the car, sliding her arms through the straps, noting that while the strain on her shoulder had dulled, it would still be problematic for flying.

She'd simply have to walk, in case she got into a situation where she had no choice, if she were going to go with what her gut was telling her.

Odson sighed, giving her a pained expression. "Kolina, I told you, we just have to wait for Jori's response. Seriously, you'll never find the lair on your own. I promise I'll take you there once he gives the 'okay'."

Kolina snorted. "First off, I'm not going to wait for any male's 'permission' if I think my daughter and dragon-sister are in danger. Second, I'm not going there—yet. I have something else to do first."

She turned her attention to Ben, who was waiting on the sidewalk. She studied him a moment as he kept his eyes on Odson's car, hand on a sleek fender. He didn't seem like the angry youth his mother had described. Maybe the last few nights had changed that.

"Where's your friend?"

Ben's gaze shot to her face. His lips thinned and eyes hardened. "Why? What's it to you?"

She shrugged. "I'm interested in the new friends you two made."

"They're not my friends." He spat.

"Oh? Hmm." She eyed him, brow lifted. "Didn't like what Darren had to say about your mother, huh?"

He snapped his head to indicate he didn't.

She swallowed the sudden rise of emotion and quickly blinked away the unexpected formation of tears.

Where the hell had that come from?

She drew a slow, deep breath.

Control.

A dozen questions rolled through her mind. Questions that she really wanted to ask another young male but couldn't.

Her gaze flicked up to Odson, who stood by, waiting with interest.

Maybe she could. Maybe one day, she could go back and find him—the young male she really wanted to talk to. The one she'd given up so very long ago.

Her thoughts flicked back to Darren. Was Darren's mother a Aeleftherian? He recognized her insignia. The angry young male, motherless with a practically absent father.

The desire to reconnect with her lost male youngling ebbed.

Coward. Her dragon said.

Yes. She agreed.

The only time she'd known real fear, was when it came to her younglings.

Kolina's drive to get to the mountain lair was more out of fear for Kymri's safety than for duty to the queen, no matter how she clung to the directive to shield her true motive.

As she stared at Ben, '*what if*' roared through her heart as she thought of the male child she'd given up.

That way lies despair.

I know.

But she couldn't help it.

Something about Ben's protective reaction to his mother triggered that longing in herself.

Aeleftherians were fiercely protective of each other.

But what would it be like to feel that strength of loyalty from a male?

Her own male youngling?

She swallowed. The decision was made a long, long time ago.

And you've paid the price since.

Yes.

And so has Kymri.

Kolina cleared her throat, wishing her dragon would go back to sleep.

Her dragon chuckled at her discomfort.

I told you so, many times.

She sighed, turning her attention back to Odson, who watched her with curiosity.

"Ben," she began, searching for the right words. "Those two males that showed up at your camp—"

"Clive and Merwin."

"Yes, stupid names," she muttered. "Clive and Merwin attacked my home. More than once. This last time, they destroyed some homes and a few of our citizens were wounded."

Ben's expression shifted from surprise to concern then settled on a deep scowl that reminded her of Odson.

"Do you know about us? Who we are?"

He nodded, his jaw tightened before he answered. "Aeleftherians. Female dragons living without males. That's why the camp exists. Males aren't allowed, so females are kicked out if they decide to keep their male babies." His tone turned accusatory.

His words impacted her like dagger strikes.

"Yes. But do you know why?"

He jerked his head.

"Our queen and her council decided long ago that we no longer wished to be subjugated to male oppression. Male dragons were incredibly domineering. We had no rights, no voices, no autonomy. So we left to create a tribe of our own. But it seemed, even removed from male influence, male younglings instinctively followed the same path. Female dragons had the same instincts and drives. The problem was—is—that full grown male dragons are much, much larger than females."

She drew in a breath, her gaze flicked between Odson and Ben.

How much to divulge?

"Aeleftheria can no longer rely on its most powerful defense—veils of myth and magnetic fields, topped up with dragon magic."

They needed help.

How many others now knew Aeleftheria's location? What were Clive and Merwin planning to do next?

"I have to stop Clive and Merwin from attacking Aeleftheria again. If they tell others where we are..." She let the thought hang between them.

"They were talking about forming a new tribe." Ben said. "On the forums."

"What forums?" Odson said.

"They got the idea from the local paranormal forum that everyone thinks is run by a crazy person. Hidden in plain sight. It's run sort of like a role play forum, but it's for real."

"Do you have access to it?" Odson asked him, stepping closer.

Ben nodded and pulled his phone from his pocket. "Here."

"Shit," Odson said after a few moments of scrolling. He looked to Kolina. "They're recruiting with Aeleftheria as the bait. Not explicitly named, but hinted at. They're keeping King Kargassa's vision alive."

"What do you mean?" Ben asked, eyes flicking from Odson to Kolina.

"It's probably the next step the king would have taken, after initiating Jori. But Jori killed those plans when he didn't submit."

"And took his place." Kolina couldn't suppress the chill that swept her body from scalp to heel. "If they come for us, we will defend to the death. If they come for us with an army, anyone that can't escape will die. We won't live under their rule."

CLIVE SURVEYED THE GROUP. One of the guys Merwin had mentioned had found an abandoned house in a seedy area of a dying town.

Half the houses here were abandoned and decaying; whatever mill had supported the community, it had shut down a decade or more ago.

This forum the young guys had set up was working, better than he could have ever imagined when he'd decided recruitment was the way to go.

As soon as they had a meeting place, males started showing up. He recognized a couple from the mountain, but most were strangers. Many were young, looking for guidance.

He grinned at Merwin, who cracked open a beer can, offering it to him.

"Not great, but not a bad start," Merwin said, picking up a second can and waving it, indicating the room in general. "I figure it won't be long before we have a better domain, what with the males that are coming in. We'll build fast."

Clive nodded, downed half the beer in a gulp, released a fizzy burp and said, "Ah, the Internet. A beautiful thing."

The sky outside the grubby windows faded to darkness quickly.

"I think this is everyone," Merwin said.

"Let's get started, then." He set the can on a nearby box and moved toward the center of the room. "Welcome! I'm Clive and this is my associate Merwin. We come from the mountain tribe ruled by King Kargassa."

The gathered acknowledged and introduced themselves.

In total, Clive counted about a dozen males of varying ages, including themselves.

"We're here to build a new tribe. Our late king had a vision for male dragon-kind. The traitorous usurper is ignorant and intent on destroying that vision. We, Merwin and I, intend to keep it alive and help it thrive. We invite you to join us."

"What's in it for us?" An older scruffy male said.

"Females. We intend to return to the old ways—bring back the old customs and traditions. Ever hear of Aeleftheria?"

A few murmured.

Someone laughed. "It's a myth."

Clive didn't take offense. He expected this. "It's real."

"You're delusional." The naysayer stood, moving toward the door.

Clive ignored the male, speaking to the rest of the gathered. "Merwin and I are looking for trustworthy dragons to help us take control of their archipelago in the coming weeks. They're a feisty flock, and I think the group of us will suffice, but we prefer a few more claws in the mix if you know some males that would like to join us."

The naysayer stopped, hand on the doorknob. "You know where it is?"

Merwin nodded. "We do."

"Where?" The male challenged; eyes narrowed.

Clive chuckled, shaking a finger. "We need trustworthy tribe brothers. We're not going to tell just anyone where our little island paradise is," he said, dropping enough hints to indicate the place existed without any clue as to where.

"What else can you tell us?" Another guy prompted.

"They're fiercely protective of their queen in her citadel."

Someone else laughed. "Like a little beehive."

"Exactly." Clive shot an arm out, pointing at the individual with a grin. "And like any hive, with a bit of planning, they can be controlled and domesticated."

"Sounds like a hassle to me," the male still standing at the door said.

Clive shrugged. "Maybe. But I'm game if anyone else is. No need to commit now. Take your time. Come back tomorrow and we'll chat some more," he said with the most magnanimous gesture he could muster. "But remember, we're only accepting like-minded male dragons. We prefer adults."

He swept his gaze over the mix of adult and youth males. "But if you prove yourself to be dependable, we'll consider allowing you to join us." His attention lingered on a few of the younger faces as he spoke. Their eyes were glued to him, sparks flaring the gears in their little minds to life as they imagined an island full of females just waiting for their arrival.

It would be a little more complicated than that, but they didn't need to know that just yet.

Chapter 9

Kolina delayed her intention to set off, yet again.

Instead, she accompanied Odson to drive Ben back to his mother at the camp. Part of her had hoped they'd pass Darren along the way, but they hadn't. She imagined he was following through with his intention to find the other males.

She didn't bother getting out of the car this time, just waited and watched the quiet camp from the front seat.

Ben and Odson stood outside Ben's home with his mother under the light of the front porch, staring down at his phone. Ben had promised to show Odson how to access the forum the males were using to communicate.

There was an obvious affection between Ben's mother and Odson.

Odson was a longtime friend. So far as friends went with Kolina. She held everyone at a distance and there were very few exceptions.

It was good he had someone here that cared about him. Someone to look after him.

Once, so very long ago, Kolina had such a special some-one—the father of her children. Too long ago. Just a shad-ow now.

She'd loved him. And left him. Twice.

It had broken her to do it. Chunks missing. Left behind when she'd reassembled herself and got on with life.

The second time, she had a daughter to focus on.

Kolina had a duty to her queen and her people. It was the Aeleftherian way.

After that, the only other man that had come close to warming her heart was Odson—when he wasn't being annoyingly obstinate.

She respected him. Cared for him, if she were honest with herself. And she wished he'd allow a mate into his life. He deserved it.

She didn't.

Her life was her duty.

Her gaze slid over Ben again.

The last time she'd seen her son, he was a little younger than Ben.

What would Kymri think, if she knew?

Would she hate me?

Kolina's vision blurred.

Her fingers slid around the locket again. Her thumb-nails slipped into the crease to slip the lock. Inside was a delicate curl of silky black hair and a tiny, pointed tip of a clipped claw.

Images of Heidi's home, filled with the scents and pho-tos of her boys and their families slammed through Kolina like a flaming boulder catapulted from a citadel tower.

She imagined herself, in a home like the Brandt's, living the family life with her son, Kymri and their father.

Would it have worked, if she'd tried?

It's too late.

She snapped the locket closed again, pressing it to her lips.

Is it?

She nodded to herself, allowing her head to fall back against the seat's head rest, eyes closed to control the tears from falling and breathing deeply to stop the telltale sniffling.

It is.

She swallowed; emotions shoved back into their steel box, she sucked in a deep breath and eased it out.

Kymri deserves to know.

She nodded again.

When this threat with the males was dealt with, she would spend time with her daughter...and talk.

The tension in her chest and shoulders eased. Lightened.

We've never done that.

First time for everything. Her dragon's voice was wry in her head.

"Shush, you," Kolina mumbled.

Finally, Odson turned from Ben and his mother, returning to the car.

He dropped onto the front seat and pulled the door closed. "We'll stop at my place to grab a few things then hit the road."

Kolina glanced out of the windshield. Ben waved to Odson then disappeared after his mother into the house.

"They're okay?"

Odson's brow lifted as he turned to look at her.

"What? As a metal dragon, I may have a heart of steel, but that doesn't mean it doesn't warm up now and then."

Odson snorted as he started the Shelby. "You're getting soft in your advanced age, Honor Guardian Steelscale."

"You already are, old man. We should set out in the morning. You need sleep and I'm still healing."

"Definitely getting soft," he muttered, throwing the car into gear.

Several of the camp residence waved as they made their way back to the road.

She shrugged. "If you say so."

THE SHELBY WAS LOADED and speeding toward the southern boundary of Black River before dawn.

"You need a new couch," Kolina muttered, sipping her coffee.

"I offered my bed." Odson threw her a wink.

"I haven't got that kind of time for dalliances. Maybe on my next vacation. Besides, you've already got a candidate and I'm not interested in complicating things for you."

"Candidate?"

"Ben's mother."

Odson snorted. "Don't listen to what Darren was saying. He doesn't know shit. Ben's mother and I care about each other, but it isn't like that. She has a wife. They asked me to come around now and then as Ben started getting older because they felt I might be a good influence on him."

"And Darren didn't know?"

"Darren's all wrapped up in himself and doesn't know anything three feet beyond his own nose."

"Sounds like most other youth I've known."

"Sounds like." He eyed her a moment. "We're really not so different, you know."

"I know. We all know. But..."

"Yeah. I understand."

"Do you? Really?"

"Believe it or not, I had a mother too. And I've lived among humans and many, many other shifters over the years. Obviously, there are differences between the sexes, but fundamentally, we're more alike than not. And ultimately. We're better off together. We balance each other."

"I know."

"Regina needs to leave her tower."

Kolina's gaze shot to Odson's profile. The sun crested the tree line, giving his complexion a golden glow.

"The council maintains the status quo. They don't allow room for change, or for going back."

"You have her ear. Talk to her."

Talk.

"And tell her what? That some ragtag camp seems to be able to make it work somehow? That's a handful; an anomaly."

He laughed. "It isn't. For all your years, you haven't seen enough of the world, Kolina."

"I've been all around the world."

"When? How long ago? When Kymri was sired? The world has changed, and continues to."

They sat in silence for another fifty miles.

"Would you want to see her? Your mother?"

His long fingers tightened on the steering wheel; the muscles in his forearms flexed.

"I have seen her. A number of times, before Elora was born. I understand she died protecting Elora and the queen and all the other Aeleftherians.."

"She was brave."

"She was. Except when it came to challenging the Queen's decision to exclude male children from island life."

Kolina swallowed. "You resent her."

"I don't want to. But yes."

"Even after all these years."

"Even so."

They stopped when the Shelby needed refueling.

"Want to drive?" Odson offered as he unwrapped a pepperoni stick he'd bought at the gas station and ate it in two bites.

"I can't drive." She wrinkled her nose at his choice of snack. "That stuff's disgusting."

He laughed, the dried meat catching in his throat, making him sputter. "You're kidding. You don't know how to drive?"

"Never had a reason to learn. Aeleftheria doesn't have vehicles. Maybe when we're done with these goons, there'll be time for fun."

"Fun. Do you even remember what that is?"

"From the way you scowl constantly, I'd have thought you'd never heard of it."

"I don't scowl," he said, brows instantly forming a 'v' on his forehead as he reached for the car door. "Come on, it will take five minutes."

"You're joking."

"Apparently not, if I've never heard of fun." He held the driver's side door open for her.

She rolled her eyes and slid onto the seat.

"Adjust the seat so you're comfortable. Levers are down below."

After a moment, she had the seat set to where she thought it should be.

He pointed at the pedals by her feet. "Brake, clutch, gas."

Then he proceeded to explain the gear shifter. Then a quick over-view on everything else she needed to know in the moment.

"I don't know about this, Odson. I might break your car." Her fingertips touched the steering wheel as her feet hovered over the pedals.

"You'll be fine; just listen, and trust me."

Kolina drew in a shaky breath. "I haven't been this nervous since my first flying lesson."

"Let me guess, plummet or fly? This isn't that scary."

"Says you," she barked.

"Relax. There aren't any other cars here." He placed a hand over hers on the gear shifter and instructed on where to put her feet.

"We have to get going, we're wasting time with this," she said after several minutes of rolling, jerking and grinding around the wide parking lot. But Odson's voice remained calm and soothing throughout his instruction. Soon, Kolina began to relax and the transitions smoothed out between gear shifts.

"Signal and watch for cars, we're getting back on the road. Relax," he said again when her shoulders bunched up to her ears.

She checked each direction of the two-lane highway four times before she allowed the car to roll through a wide turn onto the asphalt.

"That's it. Accelerate."

A car came whizzing past from behind.

"Dragonsdammit!" Kolina swore, hands clutching the wheel as Odson reached over and gently eased it so that the Shelby wouldn't veer into the ditch.

"You're fine, just keep going."

She followed every command and soon she reached third, and then fourth, gear. The discomfort of navigating the vehicle eased and she loosened her grip on the wheel.

It had taken a lot longer than the five minutes he'd estimated.

Once he was satisfied that they would stay in their lane, he pulled his phone from his pocket.

Kolina glanced over. "Jori?"

"Eyes on the road. No, I'm checking the forum Ben told us about for the address. We're not far. I just need to determine which road we turn at."

His phone chimed.

"Jori's on his way."

"What? Kymri and Elora?"

"Eyes on the road. Don't know, he didn't say. I'm letting him know where we are."

Kolina cursed again, but there was nothing more said.

As per the address and GPS coordinates, Odson guided Kolina toward a small town several miles from the main road.

The Shelby's quiet rumble drew looks as they cruised at a conservative pace down the limited main street. The town was a decrepit version of Black River. Similar styles of architecture and town planning with none of the careful maintenance. Ungroomed bushes and trees encroached over stoplights and street signs. Litter lay tossed at will along the street curbs, gathered in cracks and crumbled sidewalks.

The few residents they sighted turned to regard them with curiosity, but otherwise kept to their own business. They turned at another intersection. The streets became narrower, houses more slumped, with missing windows and boarded doors. Graffiti brightened a few, despite the lewd imagery and poor grammar.

"Drop me off here." Odson commanded. He pointed to his phone screen once she'd pulled over. "There's a chain-convenience store not far. It should be well lit. Go and wait for me there." He handed the device to her.

"Don't these guys know you? You can't go in there if they do."

"They do. But *you* sure as hell can't go. So I need you to be my backup—or getaway option when things go to crap."

"This is a terrible idea, Odson."

"Yup."

"I don't like this. Good luck."

He got out and closed the door. She watched him move around to the trunk of the car, open it and pull a few items out before closing it again.

Through the open window she said. "Really? A baseball cap and a different jacket?"

He tossed his leather coat onto the seat beside her through the passenger side window. "Clive and Merwin were the king's muscle, not brains."

He looked up and down the street before crossing and jogging further down. He turned and cast her one last glance with a jerk of his head indicating she should go.

She put the car back into gear and drove toward the location he'd indicated from his phone.

He was walking into a house full of other male dragons, meeting to discuss the seizure of her island.

As far as she was concerned, they would either accept him at his word that he wanted to join, or they would beat him to death.

Chapter 10

ODSON JERKED HIS HEAD, signaling Kolina to go.

As soon as she put the car into gear, the gentle rumble of his Shelby eased up the street then turned and soon faded.

He drew a deep breath, rolled his shoulders and walked along the dark street searching the house numbers.

If he could endure teaching Kolina how to handle his baby without losing it, he could handle anything.

The experience had had the desired effect.

She'd relaxed enough to trust him—a little more.

He just needed her to trust him a little longer.

For as long as he'd known her, she'd had a distant, reserved quality to her, but now, she was edgy and ready to spring. He understood. She carried a heavy load on her slim shoulders. He also recognized that despite their long-time friendship, part of her saw him as an enemy because of his gender; a part which was magnified now.

Odson had spent a lifetime fighting for one cause or another. Sometimes just fighting for the hell of it. But lately, he'd found himself settling in and doing what he could to be helpful. To make things right. At the camp, and with the Aeleftherians. Just for the sake of it.

I'm getting old.

And soft. His dragon chuffed.

Odson's gaze swept the street again.

Given their brief interaction with Darren, he had no doubt the kid would have made his way here through the night. Most likely hitching a ride or flying. How many of the other camp kids would have fallen for Clive and Merwin's bullshit?

He understood these kids.

Some, not all, had been abandoned by their mothers. Most of the kids that were in the camp were there because their parents wanted something better for them than where they'd originally come from.

Some were just confused, angry youth trying to navigate dragon life dominated by a human world.

And some just liked to do a little shit-kicking and face-splitting.

Odson remembered what it was like. He also remembered when he'd briefly considered having a family of his own. And why he hadn't.

The world has changed since then, and he along with it.

Who has time to settle down and have younglings when you already spend all your time rounding up outcasts?

You're too soft-hearted. His dragon said.

Not enough to go and get myself mated.

Yet.

Not gonna happen.

The inner argument ceased as he noticed a shadowy figure up the road veer toward a leaning property and go up the front steps.

Dragoness Steelscale is a desirable female.

Definitely not going to happen. Focus.

Increasing his pace, he caught sight of the figure as he disappeared into the house bearing the number he was looking for. He drew a deep breath.

Here we go.

Bounding up the stairs he caught the door before it closed and slipped inside.

"Hey." He grunted, acknowledging the male he followed in.

The unknown male nodded back.

Odson tugged the brim of his ball cap lower and rolled his shoulders to push his jacket higher so that the collar would obscure his face a little more, then sauntered in with the other late arrival.

The air was heavy with the scent of too many male dragons unnaturally crowded into the space.

A chorus of chuckles broke out on the right.

Apparently, the meeting was already in progress.

The house was dank and roughly used. Just beyond the front door was a staircase lining the left wall, then a narrow hall straight to the kitchen at the back of the house, and on the right was a front room that opened into a dining room with a wide arch dividing the spaces, also leading back.

Clive and Merwin stood just inside the room, facing the group of about a dozen males.

Odson made his way down the hall and came around to lean on the backside of the nearest arch, eyes downcast, listening.

A male seated next to the window opposite Odson spoke, "Okay, so last meeting, you said we were going to set up a new lair and take over an island that comes complete with females? Or we're taking over an island to set up a new lair that will attract females?"

Odson glanced about the room from under the rim of his cap, recognizing a few more youth from the camp. His gaze swept the rest of the group, landing on Clive and Merwin, standing at the head of the room, chests puffed, feet spread, looking like over-zealous battle commanders.

That's exactly what they think they are.

"New guy here." A familiar voice drew Odson's attention to a scruffy guy splayed on a lawn chair between the end of the semi-collapsed couch and the other side of the arch that Odson occupied. "I thought the forum said we were forming some kind of club of like-minded dragon guys that want to take their rightful place in the world. How are we supposed to do that from some island?"

Odson's eyes narrowed on the face that owned the voice.

Carson Perenga, almost unrecognizable under uncharacteristic beard growth and disheveled clothes. Agent Carson Perenga, a water dragon shifter that was created by the ocean goddess. But clearly no one else knew that because as an agent, Perenga would be less welcome at this meeting than Odson would be.

Perenga tossed Odson a grin, but quickly returned his attention to the group leaders. "Aren't we all about going public? Show the world who's king and all that? I'm down with that plan, it sucks living under the radar all the time."

Clive's complexion deepened several shades from tan to toasted. "No. We don't need to reveal ourselves to the humans." He paused for a few seconds, considering. "At least not yet."

"Why do we need this obscure island? Why don't we just go back to the mountain lair you came from and take it back?" Another male spoke up.

"Who cares, man? We're making something new here." Darren turned and snapped, "You're with us, or you're not. And if you're not, get the fuck out."

"Darren, no need to be rude, now." Merwin admonished the young male. "These are valid, though confused, questions."

Merwin took over the meeting. "We're not interested in disrupting things with the humans. We maintain the secrecy. But we want to preserve our way of life. This little island we're talking about is a hidden island in the middle of the ocean that very few know about. But *we* know where it is. And it's just occupied by a small colony of female dragons and humans." He shrugged and spread his hands. "We just figured their queen ought to have a king to rule her. Bring those females back around to the way things *should* be. They're stubborn and unreasonably defensive. They don't know any better and just need some strong males to help guide them. That's all."

Odson's lips compressed; his fist tightened against his thigh.

Kolina's steely expression popped into his mind. She was a pretty grounded individual, but he doubted even she would be able to hold her temper after that little speech.

"Whatever, I'm game. When do we leave?" Perenga said, standing, drawing everyone's attention.

Odson forced himself to relax, thinking through what Perenga was doing. Odson wasn't there to smash faces. He was there to listen and get information. If Clive and Merwin couldn't get anyone to back them, they weren't much more of a threat. But if they could get a following, they could devastate the island.

Carson Perenga would never allow that to happen any more than Odson Blackridge would.

He kept his gaze on the toe of his boot, the brim of his cap still shielding his face.

Clive chuckled. "Nice. That's what I like to see. A few more of you and we'll easily overtake the colony. No problem."

"We can go anytime. I brought some guys." Darren jumped to his feet, waving a hand toward a cluster of young males seated around him.

Merwin approached Darren, dropping a large hand on the youth's shoulder. "You sure did, and we appreciate your contributions—getting the word out and all that." He gave Darren a solid pat that jerked his slight body forward under the force of it. "We already have some important jobs for you in mind while the adults do the fighting."

"We can fight."

"Oh Yeah? Like street scuffles? Or air battles? See that scar down Clive's face? That isn't the result of no street scuffle. It took five dragoness bitches to fend him off and he's a trained warrior. And one of them managed to get a claw through his eye. Can you handle that?" he challenged.

Four. Odson knew Kolina had been the one to claw Clive's eye when she'd catapulted into him amid three guardians harrying him away from the defenseless villagers, pulling him down into the ocean, effectively ending the battle and forcing him to flee.

She'd mentioned it during the long drive.

But he maintained his silence.

"Five trained female fighters, huh? Like amazons?" Perenga prompted.

"Exactly like amazons." Clive said.

"Hey I'm all for a brawl, but how many of us are trained for combat? How many of these girl-warriors are there?"

Odson almost snickered. 'Girl-warriors.' He could imagine Kolina's teeth grinding now.

The Aeleftherian guardians were the finest warriors he'd ever seen. The only reason these males were any threat to them were because of their size and strength. Clive and Merwin had been lucky to escape with their lives.

They wouldn't on their next attempt. The guardians wouldn't try to capture for questioning, next time. They'd destroy on sight.

But still. They needed every bit of leverage they could get. And Odson was going to do that with information.

Carson clearly had his own agenda, but Odson knew that if it didn't at least align with the Aeleftherians, it wouldn't endanger them. What he wasn't sure of, was why he was encouraging them to band together. The more of them there were, the harder it would be to defend the island.

A figure slid across the darkened space outside the bare window. A subtle movement, drawing his attention to the space between this house and the next moving toward the back.

Unease prickled up his neck.

He'd caught no more than a flash of movement. A figure illuminated against the bricks of the neighboring house within the square of light cast from this room.

Kolina? He couldn't be sure.

Fuck, I hope not.

He glanced around the room, no one else seemed to have noticed the movement outside the window.

I knew it was too much to hope she'd stay away.

He turned his attention back to the conversation going on around him.

"Yeah, well if you want us to get messy with an island full of hellcats, I need a little more information than 'we're going to hit up an island and take it over', eh? What is the plan? Where are we launching from? Is this all of us? Everyone in this room? Or do you have more guys signed up?" Asked an Asian looking male with a slight Canadian accent.

"Where the hell are your balls, man? They're chicks. What's the problem?" One of Darren's friends snarled at the speaker.

"We're not here to fight each other. We're here to form a brotherhood," Clive said, sounding eerily like King Kargassa, spreading his arms and assuming an expression much like the dead king would when addressing his tribe.

Odson shuddered.

Clive was nowhere near Kargassa's charismatic stature, but he obviously was making a go of imitating him. He went on. "If you're interested in joining us, we're heading further south to meet up with more potential brothers along the way and we'll form our first council. If you want some time to think about it, you can reach us on the forum. But don't take too long, because as soon as we have enough brothers to take the island, we will."

The meeting went on for another hour, with some more challenges from the group, drawing out more information from Clive and Merwin.

They weren't as brainless as Odson had assumed them to be. They were keeping the location of the island to themselves. Probably, if they kept their smarts, right up until the last moment, so that they could maintain some sort of control. Otherwise, there was nothing stopping the males from ditching them and going off on their own, doing exactly as Merwin and Clive were doing.

Finally, the meeting began to break up and the males made their way out. The next meeting was set for the following night with the location to be communicated through the forum. Probably once they had some kind of house or building secured to meet in.

Odson listened a little longer, from his sliver of a corner behind the arch, for any useful gossip slipping between members now that the business had adjourned and social conversations dominated the space in patches.

Some of the guys that knew each other lingered in clusters, deciding their next moves. The cluster of youth from the Black River camp lounged close to wherever Clive and Merwin stood, trying to catch every bit of conversation.

He straightened and turned. Catching Perenga's eye, he nodded as he stepped back into the hall and made his way toward the front door. Just as he passed by the open arch to reach for the knob to let himself out, Darren's voice cut across the room.

"What the hell are you doing here, old man?"

Odson glanced to his left to see the youth on his feet, stalking toward him, drawing Clive and Merwin's attention.

Fuck.

He straightened and faced the remainder of the meeting attendees, his shoulders filling the width of the archway. "Just checking in to make sure you're all alright," he said, nonchalant.

"What the fuck? You think you're our babysitter or something?"

"Nope, just passing through on business. Figured I'd let your worried families know you're fine." His glance slid over the other youths. Their expressions instantly turned several shades darker, with guilty scowls. They too got to their feet.

By now, Clive and Merwin's attention were fully on Odson.

"Odson Blackridge. Outcast. Kingless. Tribeless." Clive scoffed. "Didn't think you'd be interested in what we have going on here. You made your opinions pretty clear back at the king's mountain. Last time we saw you was back in Black River running around town with the king's heir and his bitch. So, what, are you spying on us for that usurper? Traitor."

"Traitor? To whom? I've never pledged allegiance to anyone." Odson held Clive's gaze.

Clive scoffed again, stepping toward Odson, drawing back his shoulders, holding his head a little higher.

Odson wasn't sure whether to laugh or groan at his ridiculous posturing.

He knew, and Clive knew, that Clive couldn't outfight Odson if it came to it. Not on his own.

He was trying to create an air of power.

Odson cast his gaze about the room of curious onlookers then returned it to Clive and flicked it to Merwin.

Without another word, he left the ramshackle house.

Chapter 11

Kolina watched Odson stride up the slanted sidewalk as she eased the car around the corner.

Her skin itched to be leading this investigation.

Her muscles bunched, straining against the inaction. Against the secondary position. To wait. Follow. Follow Odson—a male.

She drew a deep breath and focused on driving the car.

He'd wanted her to wait at a nearby gas station.

Of course it didn't make sense for her to go into a house potentially full of male dragons. But she had to know what was going on.

Easing the Shelby to a stop two blocks from where she'd let Odson out, she parked it, turned it off and considered her options.

I can't go in but I can scout the area.

Taking the keys, she took care to lock the car as she got out and strode back in the direction to where she'd left Odson, her senses on alert in case she encountered more dragons along the way.

It wouldn't do to expose herself.

I can't remember the last time I did covert reconnaissance.

Her dragon snorted. *You've become complacent in the queen's personal guard.*

Kolina didn't argue.

It's an honor...

But we miss the action of active duty.

We do.

She slowed her pace, listening, scenting. Feeling. Her instincts awakened, giving room for her dragon to rise to the surface without shifting.

She hadn't seen which house Odson had entered.

Testing the air, she found his scent and continued moving.

The street was all shadows and slashes of dull light. Lifeless. Silent but for the distant city sounds encroaching from around the neighborhood. Like this particular district held still while the beasts converged.

Standing in the shadow of a dying tree, she waited.

Her nose wrinkled against the male scents hanging in the air.

Head tilted, she slowly turned, straining to detect male voices with her keen hearing.

Unable to catch the sounds she sought, she moved with light steps, eyes searching for glimpses of light from occupied houses.

Light, the color of cheap, tarnished gold, flashed from a front window several doors from where she stood. She crept closer.

The reek of male dragon musk increased.

So many different scents.

Her nerves tingled, muscles tightened.

Fight or flee.

She was too well trained to freeze.

With quick glances taking in her surroundings, she passed the house, eyes now focused on the front window. A heavy curtain slid aside as someone placed a beer can on the window ledge, then swung closed again, blocking the view inside the house. It was enough to catch glimpses of multiple individuals.

She moved around to the far side of the house on silent feet and hoped her own scent would dissipate before they came out. Or that their collective funk would make it impossible to detect her.

Around the back of the house, no one had bothered with heavy, light blocking curtains. She had a clear view into the rooms cramped with many dragon males. Directly across from the rear window she peered through was Odson's hunched form, with his face obscured by the ball cap he'd taken.

The voices inside were muffled. Now and then Odson tilted his head up to scan the room around him. She ducked below the window and slid past it to try to see in from the other side.

How many were in there? A dozen? More? Around the back of the house, the interior door gaped wide, and the screen door allowed the scents to ooze out of the house. She heard voices more clearly now and distinguished clips of sentences and words. She strained to hear more.

Aeleftheria...females...control.

There were two figures close to the door. She slid under the platform that extended from the door as a sort of porch, easing around trash and overgrown weeds.

"It's the same shit as last time." A male voice said.

"You think they actually know something?" The other answered.

"Hard to tell. You have any smokes?"

"Nah, just vape pods."

"If you have a spare, I'll buy it from you. I need a hit of nicotine." The first male said.

His companion chuckled. "Weird being around so many other males."

The screen door screeched open and they stepped onto the dry wood above Kolina's head, dislodging some grit.

"Thanks, man. Where you from?"

The second voice said, "who knows? The last decade or so I was out west. A friend saw the forum and told me about it, so I figured I'd check it out. You?"

The first male sighed. "Yeah, same here. I'd heard of this mountain lair full of males. But you hear all kinds of things over the years. This? This sounded new. And I'm tired of being alone, you know?"

"Sucks not belonging anywhere, but I don't know this can work. Too many guys in one place. And that bit about some paradise island full of women just waiting for us? Sounds like bullshit."

"Nah, I'm pretty sure the island is real, it's just that no one knows where it is. Except those two, apparently." He huffed.

"Think they really do?" Boots scraped the wood over Kolina's head as one of them moved.

"Dunno. Yeah? But look at those fresh scars. I'm guessing they got rejected in a bad way and are thinking to use as us an army."

Through a crack in the boards, she watched him scratch at the porch post's flaking paint.

"You good with that?"

"Not sure man, are you?" he countered.

The question remained unanswered for several moments. "I don't know. But I want to see where this goes. Hell, what have I got to lose?" He laughed. "Can you imagine one of *them* as a king?"

They both chuckled.

"Only until they got us to that island. Anyway, we'll find out soon enough. I think they're getting ready to launch soon."

"We have enough guys now?"

"Depends on if everyone's on board. I don't know that everyone is. I don't know that I am." He snorted, taking a long drag on the vape pod.

"Why not?"

"I think they're about done their intro spiel. I'm going back in to see if they're going to give us any more information."

Kolina waited until they'd both gone inside before crawling out from under the porch and moved around the house, completing the perimeter. She could see nothing more and couldn't hear what was being said inside the house.

She returned to the Shelby, thinking about what she'd overheard.

Was any of it useful?

At least two of these males were drawn out of curiosity. They lacked the fervor she'd expected from males.

They sounded lonely.

They didn't have much faith in Clive and Merwin.

But none of that meant they weren't a danger to Aeleftheria.

An apathetic enemy was still an enemy.

Would Odson tell her anything more than she'd just learned herself?

He knew where the island was. He knew how they operated, what their defenses were.

Odson appeared to be shielding his identity when she'd glimpsed him.

But given that he was in a house full of other males, what would stop him from stepping into the position that Clive and Merwin were setting up for themselves?

He wouldn't do that.

Would he?

A gathering of males. A great opportunity for a strong and clever leader.

Odson was strong and clever.

Surely, he'd have had the opportunity over the long years. Unless he'd been waiting for something. Or someone with a legitimate claim to rule?

Sighting the bright lights of the gas station, she parked the car around the side of the store and got out.

I need to think.

She paced.

"I still have no information on Kymri and Elora," she growled.

Odson insisted they were safe with Jori Mountainside.

The stench of male musk lingered in her nose, making it difficult to concentrate on anything other than the knowledge that a large group of males were gathering to attack her home.

It didn't matter who was leading them or who would end up as king. They knew where the archipelago was and they were preparing to attack soon.

Still faced with the same question, Kolina considered her options: Alert Aeleftheria and help them prepare, or wait and gain more information.

The Aeleftheria information relay system was archaic, but it had to be, with the magnetic and magical barriers that protected the archipelago.

It wasn't like she could just call the island.

They did have a relay system. Step one. But it would still take time.

Standing on the far side of the Shelby, she glanced down into the car. Odson's phone was still there. He'd left it unlocked so that she could use the map system.

She quickly retrieved it from the seat and determined how to contact someone.

In moments, she'd found Heidi Brandt's number and hit the dial icon.

Relief shot through her when Heidi's voice came through the device.

"Odson?"

"Heidi, it's Kolina. I need you to contact Aeleftheria, can you get a message out for me?"

"Of course."

KOLINA LEANED ON THE fender of the Shelby as she waited for Odson to return. By the time he came into view, she'd settled on her course of action.

"We're heading south," he said, opening the driver's side door.

"Gas tank is full and there are more snacks in the backseat." She joined him in the car and a moment later they were moving.

She studied the tight muscles in his face. "When are they attacking?"

He glanced at her. "That was risky, you know. Going to the house."

So he had seen her.

"I don't think anyone else saw you. But I did pick up your scent on my way back. Too risky, Kolina. You should have just trusted me."

"Trust?"

He let out a heavy sigh as his thumbs whapped the steering wheel, thrumming his frustration. "Yes. Trust. Me. I'm trying to help you. You can't go through life trusting only other Aeleftherians. Your network of allies will collapse if you don't trust them. And I'm your ally."

"Other than a handful of souls, I don't trust anyone, Od-son. How have *you* survived this long trusting everyone you meet?"

He shot her a glance at her derisive tone. He didn't bother explaining himself, which she appreciated.

"They're continuing to rally as they head south. No launch point given but I would suspect it's somewhere near Charleston."

She nodded. That was where Jori Mountainside had launched his plane from.

She replayed the conversation she'd overheard. Two lonely males.

Glancing at Odson again, she considered him a few moments. "Why aren't you part of a tribe? You could be a king."

He grunted a laugh. "Too much work to be king. Ask Jori. Why I'm not in a tribe?" He shrugged. "Long story."

"We've got time."

He shook his head, eyed her, then said, "Trust, Kolina."

It was her turn to grunt as she turned her face toward the passenger window. The darkness made it so that there was nothing to see but her own reflection in the glass.

Trust.

A double-edged concept in her world.

Aeleftherians had to trust one another to survive. Their ecosystem was small, their defenses limited and their allies very carefully selected. And yet, when she thought of her sisters, who among them did she trust? Truly trust? With her inner self?

Launia was the closest person she had to a friend on the island.

She counted Heidi Brandt as a friend. Heidi made it hard not to.

She'd spent the measure of her existence building and strengthening her walls of steel.

We've done as we've had to in order to protect ourselves.

Kolina agreed with her dragon.

To the detriment of our relationship with Kymri.

This has been unfortunate. I told you it didn't have to be this way.

You did.

But you were afraid.

Yes.

We must fix this.

I don't know how.

We must open our heart a little and learn to trust a little more.

She cast another glance to Odson. One of the very few males, that she knew of, that had been to the island more than once.

"How did you learn the location of the island?"

"I didn't."

She laughed. "You don't know where it is? I thought you came and went as you pleased."

He shook his head.

A deep pit began to open in her gut. Her earlier suspicions gnawing at the edges of her fears for her island.

Was he following events with the males in order to learn its location?

"I don't need to know where it is, Kolina. I'm content traveling under the same requirements as everyone else. Blindly."

"I don't believe you." She blurted, then flinched.

He chuckled. "Your diplomacy still needs work. You don't need to believe me."

"Why? Why wouldn't you want to know?"

"Why do I need to?" He countered. "I have no desire to live there permanently, as lovely a place as it is. There is nothing about it that says 'home' to me. And there is no one there to make me want to stay." This last he said with the weight his full gaze on her face.

She shivered.

"No one?"

He turned his attention back to the road. "Not without trust."

Her heart pounded in her chest as a fissure sliced through a section of the steel wall.

But memories of their pairings over the years tumbled through her mind. Casual. Mutual physical gratification.

Any time she'd ever had thoughts of more creep in, they'd been quickly cut down.

Dangerous.

I promised never to allow myself into a position to get my heart ripped apart again.

We broke our own heart. For duty. No one did this to us.

It doesn't matter.

She didn't like examining her own loneliness.

It was nothing but a waste of time, and a distraction from what was important. The protection of her queen and her people.

Her home.

Is it?

Home?

She swallowed. It is what it is.

She cast Odson another glance. "How is life in Black River?"

He shrugged.

"Is it your home now?"

"For now."

"How do you decide?"

"I don't."

She considered this. "What does that mean?"

"Either it feels like a home, or it doesn't. And for me, that always comes down to the people around me in a given place."

"The Brandt family."

He nodded. "And the camp. That's all they're trying to do. Live in peaceful coexistence and build a home for their families. That's all."

She'd always thought that for those that chose to leave Aeleftheria, that it was about defiance to the Aeleftherian way of life. She supposed it could be both. The council believed it was about power. But then, the council believed everything was about power. Everyone outside—and within Aeleftherian—wanted to control the queen and the island.

The way they try to control her.

Past experience had proven that.

She studied Odson's profile in the darkness of the car. Really studied him.

They'd known each other for so very long. He'd never done a deed or said a word to indicate he was ever interested in power, or dominance or control.

He is a free spirit. Living as he chooses.

He rejected the mountain tribe and their king.

It was time she removed her blinders and examined her biases. Being off island and away from the reinforcement of her social norms, it was a little easier to even consider doing so.

Otherwise, why would she need to?

Because we are no longer content with life as it is. Her dragon said.

No. We are not.

It's time to change.

The council will see treason if I try.

We both know the queen knows it's time.

Nothing will change until she decides it will be so. And I won't abandon my people. They are still in danger, even if the danger may not be from every direction of the compass. One is enough.

She turned her body so that her shoulder rested against the door of the car and faced Odson more. Opening to him, a little more.

Maybe he had secret designs to get the location of the island and rule it for himself.

But, as she regarded him while he drove, the thought was ludicrous.

Not impossible, she conceded.

It was the fear of an over-cautious closed society, to see enemies in every outsider's face.

Her mounting paranoia was absurd.

She realized if she wanted to build bridges, she had to participate from her side of the wall.

"It's a long drive, and while I generally don't mind silence, I'm tired of it just now."

The corner of his mouth lifted. "What do you want to talk about?"

"I have no idea, to be honest."

"I'm always honest."

"So am I. I just..."

"Omit things."

"Yes," she said. Then stepped to the edge of her wall. "It gets tiresome, being guarded. All the time."

He spared her a glance. "It does."

They started with the little things. Sharing bits and pieces of common experiences until they decided to find a hotel for a few hours of rest before continuing on to the next meeting place.

Chapter 12

MERWIN SCROLLED THROUGH THE forum discussions. He looked up as Clive entered the motel room carrying a bag and a tray with drinks.

"How's the activity?" Clive asked nodding toward Merwin's phone.

"More and more males are signing up, but not all of them participate in the conversation. Most lurk."

"What are we going to do about Blackridge?"

Merwin shrugged. "What's there to do? So what if he's trying to mother a bunch of kids that don't want him around? He can't stop us. Even if he tried, he's just one male. With as many followers as we have now, he'd be easy to take down."

Clive grunted. "He's a good fighter."

Over the years, they'd both witnessed what he was capable of.

"Not against all of us."

"He might warn the island. The kid, Darren, said he saw Odson with an Aeleftherian in Black River."

Merwin shrugged. "So? They're already defensive. A warning would make no difference. And they're so isolated, there's no one around to help them—if there were anyone that would."

"It's too bad Kargassa didn't have the chance to lead the attack himself."

Merwin didn't respond to Clive's adoration of their late king, who had done little for the tribe. He was all about his own power and glorification. But, Merwin was ambitious and moving up through the ranks of the king's guard had granted him some nice perks, even if he had to follow someone else's orders.

"We'll bring those females back to their proper place." He reached for the offered coffee.

He just had to bide his time. It was very likely not every male that flew out with them would survive. Not if their last attempt was any indication. Those females would fight tooth and claw. The little bitches had near-ly ripped his wings to shreds and drowned Clive.

They were lucky to have escaped with their lives.

What they needed was the technology the king used to subdue females. The collar he'd created to enslave the Aeleftherian ambassador was a useful tool.

That was a little something Merwin was working on, on the side.

He'd contacted the wizard who'd created the collar that Kargassa had used to suppress the ambassador's magic, locking her in her human form. There had also been a set of wrist shackles used to bind the usurper's female.

Having escaped from the mountain, he no longer had access to what was left of the manacles, collars and whatever other devices the dead king had made. He'd have to have his own made and be taught the spells.

Doing it himself ensured he was the one in control since the only one that could unlock a device was the one that cast the spell on it. Which also meant he'd be the one controlling the female population—once they got them subdued enough to shackled them.

That was the tricky part.

"Listen, I have a contact I'm going to meet with. He's working on a special weapon for us." He leveled his gaze on Clive, watching his predictable reactions.

Clive's brows went up, then dropped into a frown. "Just text him to come to us, we're busy recruiting for a raid here."

"Clive, this is something I need to do in person. You can handle the riffraff that show up to the meetings. It's not like we're cherry picking the fodder for the attack. You're great at convincing the other guys how lucky they are for the chance to join us and blah blah," he lied.

"Yeah? You think so? I have been practicing my speeches. I think they're getting better."

He sure had been practicing, and driving Merwin nuts. But it didn't matter. Thanks to the forum, word was getting out fast. That was enough for their needs. But Clive needed the ego stroke and the sense he was leading.

"Yep. You got this."

"Awesome. You make a great second man, Merwin. Exactly the kind of adviser a king needs."

Merwin cringed as he sipped his coffee and mumbled. "Thanks man. I'm leaving before the meeting. I'll meet you in Charleston in time for takeoff, don't worry."

"Who's your contact? I may know him."

"Doubt it. Buddy from years back," he lied again. "Name's Conrad."

Clive shook his head, as Merwin had expected.

"Powerful guy?"

"Very."

"Good, good we need more guys like that. Alright, I'm going to get some shut-eye to heal up some more before the big day."

Merwin nodded. "I'm going to monitor the forums and do a little research."

Clive disappeared into the washroom and Merwin turned his attention back to his phone to confirm his meeting with the conjurer that would make him king.

KOLINA REACHED FOR A towel as she stepped out of the shower.

It was pure bliss to stand under the hot waterfall after being confined to Odson's car for what felt like an ice age. Too eager for the warm shower, she'd forgotten to bring fresh clothes into the bathroom with her.

She dried her hair and body with the towel, then wrapped and secured it around her torso.

Wiping the condensation from the bathroom mirror, she considered her reflection as she dragged her fingers through the tangles in her hair. The brush was also with her clothes, but she'd have to do this anyway. May as well revel in the few more minutes alone, in the balmy steam-clouded warmth.

Odson.

They held a mutual physical attraction that one or the other would pursue over the years. Not often, because the time between meetings could span years or decades. Nor were they exclusive.

She stepped out of the steamy bathroom to retrieve her forgotten clothes.

Odson stood with arms crossed in the middle of the small room, watching the news on the television. "Storm rolling in," he commented, sparing her a glance, then another, lingering on her eyes.

She held his gaze.

Moving three steps forward to the end of the bed, next to where her clothes lay abandoned, her gaze remained transfixed on his.

He stared back through thick black lashes that framed slate gray irises.

Kolina always admired how beautiful Odson's eyes were. Especially the rare times he smiled.

A sharp knock on the door broke the spell with a snap.

Snatching her clothing from the bed, she went back to the bathroom. She hesitated, with her hand on the doorknob, meeting his twinkling eyes.

He smiled and waved her away. She smiled back.

The second knock on the hotel room door had her shutting herself away in the bathroom to dress.

Muffled voices filtered through the thin door, male and female.

Familiar.

Shoving her feet into her jeans and yanking her shirt down over her head, she opened the door.

Kymri stared back at her. She stood next to the bed, hand on Kolina's backpack. Jori and Elora stood at ease next to Odson, just inside the door. Another unfamiliar man was with them.

Kolina had never been the emotional doting mother. She was too hard for that.

As she held her daughter's uncertain but direct gaze, her heart flipped several times.

Kymri was safe. The baby was safe.

Kolina's arms lifted of their own accord, reaching for her adult daughter to hug her in a way she hadn't hugged her since she was a youngling. She didn't miss Kymri's shocked expression before she embraced her rigid form.

After a few seconds, Kymri relaxed, her arms encircling Kolina in return.

Once Kolina had released her daughter, ignoring the gathered tears in her eyes, she turned on Jori. "You shouldn't have kept her from communicating with me. I would have gone to the mountain to fetch her and Elora back to Aeleftheria." Her voice was hard. Accusatory.

"He did no such thing," Elora said, stepping toward Kolina.

Kolina's gaze flicked to the ambassador, back to Jori's flushed face, then returned to Elora. "And you. You have a lot to answer to the queen about."

Her sustained worry and anger and frustration found an outlet on the queen's close friend and trusted ambassador, who'd gone missing decades ago.

The two women stared at one another from opposite sides of decades' old choices.

Kolina had given up her own son and a life of domestic happiness to toe the line of duty to their queen and Aeleftherian social responsibility.

Elora had abandoned her queen and people for a chance at a life with her son and lover.

The fact that that life was stolen from her by the dragon king, Richmund Kargassa, Jori's natural sire, didn't ease Kolina's resentment. Not in that moment.

Jaw clenched, Kolina regarded her Aeleftherian sister, holding back her judgment.

And yet, in all those years of captivity, Elora had never given up her son or her queen and people.

Respect and resentment warred within Kolina's chest.

"There's a coffee shop around the corner." Odson said, breaking the tension. "We should talk."

She turned on Odson, the earlier spell she'd fallen into gone cold. "This is Aeleftherian business."

"No, mother, this is Dragon business," Kymri said, placing a hand on Kolina's shoulder.

Kolina spun toward Kymri.

Kymri stood straight, resolute, ready for battle, expression identical to the one she wore before every patrol.

As a guardian commander, she'd had to be ready for anything, storms, attacks, accidents—anything could happen anytime.

Kolina realized Kymri usually wore that expression—or one of wariness—when she faced Kolina.

Flashes of Heidi Brandt and her family, the camp residents and even her earlier ease with Odson tumbled through her mind.

It doesn't have to be this way.

Eternally defensive. Constantly suspicious. Living on the verge of battle.

All the time.

With everyone she knew.

Her gaze flicked from person to person standing before her. Five sets of eyes, watchful, wary, resolute.

She stepped back and released her pent breath.

Allies, Kolina. Not enemies. Her dragon soothed her anxiety.

We've been living too long as though everyone is an enemy, even among friends.

Yes.

Time to change? Can I? Kolina wondered.

Depends on how much you want it.

I don't know how.

They will help us.

Kolina reached for her jacket, which also lay discarded next to her backpack. To Kymri she nodded. "Dragon business. Let's go talk."

Chapter 13

KOLINA WATCHED JORI CAREFULLY manage the hot drinks as he carried them from the cafe counter to their table. She'd been introduced to Jonathan Mountainside during the short walk. Elora's human husband and Jori's stepfather. Father. Kargassa was Jori's sire. He'd never been a father to him.

Much like she hadn't been a mother to her son.

She shoved that thought aside and cleared her throat. "So why didn't you just text Odson so I could meet you at the Mountain lair? And where is Marli? Has she returned to Aeleftheria?"

A smile quirked the corner of Elora's mouth as she and Kymri exchanged glances.

"In our absence, Marli is our Aeleftherian representative at the mountain lair." Kymri said. "The, uhm, internet was down. The phone and satellite too."

Kolina blinked, waiting for an explanation.

"They accidentally got knocked out." Elora added.

"What happened? A storm? Must have been quite the storm to have cut communications for so long."

"Not exactly." Kymri lifted her shoulders, not meeting Kolina's eyes. Instead, her gaze slid to Jori, her smile widening.

"What?" he asked, glancing up from his careful navigation so as not to spill the drinks.

Kymri shrugged, looking innocent. "Nothing."

"We were just trying to explain to Kolina why we hadn't communicated before now."

Jori's eyes flicked back to Kymri, a frown slammed into place. "You threw me under the bus, didn't you? We agreed we wouldn't tell her what happened."

Kymri laughed, raising her hands. "I didn't tell her, I promise!"

"I bet I can guess what happened," Odson said, setting a plateful of pastries on the table next to the steaming mugs. He straightened, looking at Jori. A grin slowly split his face.

"Dude, come on!" Jori's eyes darted to Kolina and back to Odson, pleading. "Don't do this to me, *uncle* Odson."

Odson chuckled at Jori's obvious discomfort, then shrugged and took the seat between his sister Elora and Kolina.

"I'd almost forgotten you two were siblings," Kolina murmured, regarding Odson and Elora.

Jori settled between Kymri and Elora, almost directly across from Kolina at the table.

"So, what happened? Did you try to tinker with it and broke it instead?" Didn't men like to tinker with things? She'd been told, at some point in her long past, that it was a male trait.

"Not exactly," Kymri hedged again, laughing outright at Jori's warning growl.

"Well, I made no such promises of secrecy," Elora announced. She turned to Kolina with a mischievous glint in her eyes, leaning to pick up her coffee and sip.

Kolina was on edge waiting for someone, anyone, to answer the dragonsdammed question.

"Good coffee," Elora murmured, setting her mug down gingerly. "My son, new to his dragon as he is, is still learning to fly."

"He's a wonderful flyer," Kymri cut in.

"It's the landings that need work," Odson said.

"You guys are killing me." Jori, rigid on his seat, didn't meet Kolina's face. His cheeks were flushed a deep red. "You're not supposed to let your girlfriend's mother know about shit like that."

Laughter erupted from Kolina, head thrown back, hand to her chest.

"Great." Jori grumbled.

Kolina laughed harder as she imagined what must have happened.

Tears streamed from her eyes as the weeks of tension finally found release.

All she'd known was that Kymri and Elora were alive at the king's mountain lair, and that the king was dead.

And that apparently Jori was the heir, which meant, he was now king.

"Fledgling dragons are the most fun to watch when learning to fly," she gasped. "So gangling and awkward. Crashing into things, unable to navigate."

If he was the heir and he had killed his sire, he must be a magnificent dragon indeed.

A dragon powerful enough to take the island, should he want to.

She struggled to control her laughter. "And here, all this time, I feared you were going to head an army to subdue and take control of Aeleftheria. It never occurred to me you would need to learn to fly first." She wiped tears from her cheeks.

Jori stared at the ceiling, mortified.

Jonathan, Elora and Kymri tried to disguise their amusement with sips from their mugs.

Odson grinned at his nephew.

Once she got her laughter under control, she reached across the table, placing a hand on Jori's. "I haven't laughed like that in...a very long time." She drew in a deep steadying breath and eased it out. "I'm just glad you're all safe. That has been my main concern. But I am pleased to hear you have discovered your dragon and are learning to fly."

She pressed her lips together lest another eruption of laughter escape, and quelled the periodic urge to giggle by sipping her drink as the others had done.

On the tabletop, Odson's phone buzzed, drawing everyone's attention.

He picked it up, checked the message and grunted. "Cavalry are here."

"Cavalry?" Kolina asked. "We're dragons, we don't need horses."

"It's an expression, mother." Kymri said.

The bell above the cafe door jangled as two more patrons entered the establishment.

Odson's usually stoic face lit with a grin. He got to his feet, extending a hand in greeting.

Kolina turned to see the newcomers.

"Carson Perenga and Bai Yun Long. I haven't seen you in...how long?" Her mouth hung open studying the faces of the male dragon shifters. Carson was a water dragon and Bai Yun an air dragon from the far east.

"An eternity. Bayn Long." Bai Yun said, introducing himself to Jori, Kymri and Jonathan.

"Good to see you're all intact since I saw you a few months ago," Carson said to Kymri and Jori. "And Elora. I'm glad the rumors of your continued existence are true. Kolina Steelscale, always a pleasure."

Everyone seemed genuinely pleased to see everyone else.

Jori stood. "Drinks are on me, what can I get you both?"

Carson and Bayn named their drinks with thanks and the group rearranged their tables and seating to accommodate the extra bodies.

The tiny cafe, full of old dragons, was starting to get a little cramped.

There was Dragon business to discuss.

MERWIN ADJUSTED THE BACKPACK slung from his shoulder as he cast furtive glances around the dark alley he had chosen to receive the portal.

As soon as he'd ensured privacy, he texted his coordinates.

Moments later a portal opened to a dark, cluttered room where his contact awaited.

With final glances toward exposed directions, Merwin stepped through the portal and into the conjurer's space.

"Conrad," Merwin acknowledged as he stepped into the room, taking in his surroundings with further quick glances to ensure they were alone.

"Dragon." Conrad replied, flicking his hands toward the portal, causing it to collapse.

The sudden change in atmosphere tickled Merwin's eardrums. He swallowed to relieve the pressure.

Merwin straightened his shoulders, regarding his contact.

Either he was going to get what he wanted, or he'd made himself stupidly vulnerable.

Conjurers couldn't be trusted unless you had the payment they wanted and could ensure its defense—in case they tried to just take it from you.

He'd clearly walked into a spellcaster's domain.

Dragons paid little attention to most other predators. But even against adult male dragons, conjurers could be dangerous.

"You've brought the payment." Conrad said.

Merwin nodded and pulled a small cloth bag from a compartment on the front of his backpack, then replaced it out of view.

"Good. Let's get started. I've had to do some refresher research into this spell considering how long it's been since the last time I used it." He moved toward a large book set upon a heavy wooden table in the center of the room. The stone walls were lined with shelves that were crammed with all manner of items from bottles in various states of use, to scrolls, books and other random things.

Things Merwin hadn't seen in centuries. Things he was sure were long extinct—dried and encased in glass or suspended from the ceiling. He shuddered, recognizing bits and pieces of petrified anatomy.

"In fact," Conrad continued, as he rearranged several bottles, boxes, bowls and herb bundles closer to the book he was focused on. "The last time I worked this spell was for your king. Kargassa."

"Late king. He's dead."

Conrad lifted a brow. "Interesting. I hadn't heard. My condolences." He bowed his head, but his voice lacked sincerity. "And you are pursuing some of his secrets."

"Focus on the spell. As you said, your time is short, as is mine."

Conrad shrugged, but he hadn't stopped moving, adding ingredients to a cauldron set within reach. "As I'm sure you know, you can entrap anything with this spell. Anything but me, of course. Built in failsafe. You never know when a client might have designs on a powerful conjurer such as myself." He chuckled. "Though it will work on other conjurers."

Merwin maintained his silence, watching the spell caster at work. He understood none of what he did and didn't care.

"Vessel of choice? Whatever it is, it will affect the ratio of ingredients."

Merwin moved his backpack over and set it on the edge of the table, unzipping it. Inside, he pulled dozens of thin metal bracelets designed to fit a woman's wrist.

Conrad whistled. "That must have cost you. Titanium? And so many."

"They'll work?"

"Anything will work. The first item I ever used this spell on was a golden lamp. The spell is powerful enough to have entrapped a Djinn in that lamp. And dragons with iron collars and manacles, as your king saw fit to use. Titanium bracelets will work equally as well."

"And I am the only one that can release the spell."

"That's right. Either by speaking the necessary incantation, or by death. The former is usually preferred by the client."

Merwin ignored the attempt at humor. "Usually? How many other clients do you sell this spell to? Who are they?" his shoulders tightened.

"As I said, I haven't conjured this spell in some time."

Merwin noted how Conrad evaded answering the question.

He considered the price he'd bartered for the spell and enchanted items. Was it worth it?

He wasn't so sure. A vein in his temple began to throb, his chest tightened as doubt set in.

Had Merwin made a mistake and walked into a trap?

No, he'd already considered this, and decided this was the correct course of action for his plans. It was the confinement of the magic practitioner's work-room. It reminded him too much of one of the dungeon cells in the base of the mountain lair. His eyes darted around the claustrophobic room. There were no windows, and his senses told him they were deep underground.

Among the myriad of scents of old and musty ingredients was the scent of new decay. Recent death. His gaze flicked about the room again.

Was there even a door? There were no breaks between the shelves surrounding them. The floor was solid stone. Glancing up, the ceiling was all heavy beams, and he could detect no trap door.

Sweat prickled his scalp.

Did Conrad portal here?

Merwin forced his shoulders to relax. So long as the room wasn't magically warded against dragons in some way or another, he could simply shift and break free.

I hope.

Deciding to set the concern aside, he focused on what the conjurer was doing.

This was it. He'd had to gather as many of these bracelets as he could, unless he sought out Conrad's magic again in the future, but he'd rather not.

The less contact the better, lest he put himself in a position of vulnerability. He was well aware that dragon pieces were valued among spell casters.

Hence the payment.

Dragon scales.

If he'd been at the mountain lair, he could have simply gone to the aerie or the training pits and collected some naturally discarded scales from those places. No longer accessible, it was no longer an option.

He'd had to resort to sacrificing some of his own.

He just hoped the risk was worth it. He couldn't be sure the wizard wouldn't just use the scales to ensnare him.

The irony wasn't lost on him.

It is necessary. There is no other way to ensure long term victory.

None that he could see, and time was running out because they'd set the course to go after the females as soon as possible, rather than wait another eternity. Momentum was gathering with these forum followers, and they had to strike while interest was piqued.

Neither he nor Clive were interested in the long game. Not anymore. Not now that they knew where the island was. The females would be on full alert, sure, but they too would have had little time to strengthen their island defenses or bring in allies—if they had any.

Shock and awe.

Come in early, hit hard, suppress and shackle. Simple. No screwing around.

He eyed the bracelets. With no idea how many drag-onesses there were on the island, he would have to be smart about how he used them.

The stronger ones. The important females.

The queen. The fighters—the guardians.

Enough to make them vulnerable. Vulnerability brought control.

The hardest part would be getting the shackle in place while they were in human form.

Figure that part out later.

Conrad periodically cast him furtive glances from the corner of his eye as he worked.

Was he planning to entrap him after all?

Maybe he should destroy the wizard after he complet-ed the incantation and taught him the final part of the spell.

I haven't eaten anyone in a while.

He eyed the wizard.

Not much meat on his bones. He'd be more crunchy than tasty.

He'd heard wizards were bitter and caused indigestion.

Merwin shrugged, determined to see this through. He'd eat him if he had to.

He flicked another glance toward the ceiling then along the floor searching for wards.

If there were any, they were well concealed.

Something out of place caught his attention.

Is that a shoe?

"Who's that?" Merwin nodded in the direction of the exposed footwear still attached to a woman. The rest of the body had junk dumped on her—no, no, she looked as though she'd been thrown into the corner and stuff fell on top of her. Other parts of her were visible now that he paid closer attention. Dead eyes stared out at him from a gap between an upended box and bundles of dried herbs.

Conrad didn't bother to look at what Merwin was referring to. "Owner of this place."

"Huh. And here I thought this classy place was yours." Merwin shrugged. It was none of his concern who this place actually belonged to as long as he got what he wanted.

Conrad held up a vial, measuring drops of some oily liquid that gave off a foul odor. "No one sees my place on the first date." He grinned and winked at Merwin.

Conrad's work went on for almost an hour before he reached for the bracelets and dropped them into the cauldron with the other ingredients. The wizard's hands glowed as he worked up to the last part of the spell with a dramatic flash.

"Is that flash bang a natural cause, or just a dramatic flourish?" Merwin asked.

Conrad ignored the question, scooping the metal circlets out of the cauldron and dumped them back into Merwin's pack before he zipped it closed.

"The enchantment is complete. I'll teach you the binding and release spells. You'll have to commit it to memory. I don't make cheat sheets."

He ran through the spell, which contained several verses, a number of times with Merwin, until he was sure he'd remember them.

"I've got it."

"Remember, the item can only be used once. The binding imparts the properties of the first part of the spell to fuse with the bearer. When the incantation is dispelled, it also breaks the magical fusion. The item would have to be prepared anew." Conrad pulled the spell book from the table, tucking it away in a messenger bag that had been set aside.

Merwin nodded. This information confirmed his need to be very careful of who he selected to shackle.

"The scales requested as payment." He handed the bundle over to Conrad, who opened the sack and extracted a few.

Another shiver rippled down Merwin's spine. Those were his scales in Conrad's hands.

"What will you use them for?"

Conrad's rapt attention flicked to Merwin's face. A smile touched his lips. "They're yours?"

Merwin didn't like the glint in the wizard's eyes.

"Various spells. Don't worry, dragon. I am no threat to you."

Like hell.

With Conrad's eyes glued to Merwin's face, he was able to read the dragon's expression the second Merwin thought Conrad was indeed a threat.

Conrad waved his arms, muttering several words, and cast two portals which opened with a hiss. He grasped the bag of dragon scales to his chest and stepped back into the one that opened behind him. He nodded toward the other that opened to the alley Merwin had come from.

"Good luck, dragon." Conrad grinned at him from the safe side of his portal, which looked like another city. There was nothing notable to identify where it was, just an alley, identical to his own except for the dirty snow coating the ground.

Merwin snatched his pack of manacles from the table and stepped through his own portal. "Good doing business with you, wizard." He vacated the spell room, returning to the dark alley. The portal disappeared with a low boom. He gave his head a shake trying to dislodge the pressure in his eardrums again.

He was alone in the dank space of the alley, except for a rat scurrying in search of his dinner.

Merwin slung the pack over his shoulder. Next phase done. Now, they just had to prepare the troops.

He started walking.

A grin stretched his mouth. "Those bitches have no idea what's coming."

Turning the corner, he strode toward the busier area of the neighborhood, which led to the motel.

He just had to remind Clive to control his violent impulses outside of battle.

Most dragonesses didn't submit to such base displays of physical dominance. It had the opposite effect, causing them to dig their claws in and snap back with sharp teeth.

Unreasonable. Like spitting, hissing cats, ready to shred an opponent's face with a turn of mood. Not that such behavior made Merwin wary, it was simply a waste of time. His time.

Time better spent solidifying their position to rule the island.

He joined a crowd of pedestrians at an intersection, then crossed, then crossed again.

The males had spent decades—centuries even—following Kargassa's rule. Long enough to learn manipulation and conditioning.

Guys like Clive believed the shit Kargassa fed them to keep himself in power.

Merwin never had. He reaped the benefits of working for Kargassa but he'd always had his own agenda. As did many others in the lair.

Others that had left, seeing the chaos coming with the new usurper taking over, and others that stayed, looking for opportunities.

Merwin and Clive had left out of necessity. To stay at the mountain would have been to do so under a long, long reign of imprisonment.

They'd attacked the heir's woman and threatened his mother.

That wouldn't go unpunished.

Chapter 14

"YOU'RE SURE THEY WON'T shift?" Jori asked again.

"Yes." Kolina said. "No one wants to risk that kind of exposure to the humans."

They sat in a car Jori had rented to make the drive to meet with them. Jori, Kymri, Jonathan and Elora had flown by plane from the mountain to the coast, then driven the rest of the way.

Jori's lack of dragon flight skills were still a concern, and Kymri's ability to shift during pregnancy was also severely limited.

"I will help you learn to fly and land," Kolina said.

He shrugged. "This whole dragon thing is still very new to me."

She studied his bearded face a moment. Jori Mountainside, the tattoo-covered adventurer. He released the elastic holding the thick hair from his face, tamed it with long fingers and wound it into a bun at the back of his head.

Bound to her daughter.

An adventurer, not a warrior.

Was Kymri training him?

"You risk losing control of the mountain lair by coming here, Jori."

He blew out a breath. "Things there are definitely...complicated. Eamerson and Stenlen are overseeing things right now. I guess there's a whole faction that believe in the right of rule by bloodline." He shrugged. "I don't understand it."

"And the other factions?"

"Probably considering their options. I gave them time to decide. Stay or go." He shrugged again and sipped from the bottled water he'd brought with him. "I was never cut out to lead a lair of dragons. Never in my wildest dreams could I have imagined life going in this direction."

"So, why are you doing it?"

"I've never let anyone push me into doing anything I didn't want to do, in the past. This is different. Kymri and my mother's lives are at risk if I don't. The safety of Aeleftheria. If I don't try to do something about it, then that makes me a shitty human."

Kolina smiled, but it was bittersweet. "I may have misjudged you."

"Most people do," he said, matter of fact.

She studied him a moment longer. Dragon life was long. Centuries, millennia long.

Time was usually meaningless.

Until it no longer was.

Although Jori was dragon born, he was everything that defined a human. He lived to experience life. Be in it, part of it. *Be* it.

Is that what attracted Kymri to him?

He represented the world, here and now. Not what was, centuries ago.

He seemed to be trying to bring his modern ideals and values to the male dragon world.

Trying to change the things that were wrong. The things that had divided dragon society a part in the first place.

Is he strong enough?

Or were they all kidding themselves? Was it just in their nature to want to dominate?

For Kolina, the majority of her life had been spent under this shroud of threat.

Males were never to be fully trusted.

Her children's sire hadn't even been a dragon. Could he still be alive?

Kolina's gaze returned to Jori again and again.

"I can feel your curiosity. Go ahead, ask away," he said, turning his gaze from the window to look at her.

A smile tugged at her lips, but she didn't apologize.

"You and Kymri."

He nodded, turning in his seat to face her properly. "The baby?"

"Yes."

"There hasn't been a lot of time to discuss all of this, we've had a lot on our plate. But, regardless, we would work things out to the child's benefit—always."

Kolina smiled. "Kymri seems to have found a rare gem."

If he spoke truthfully.

"I'm not," he said. "Unique. I'm more common than you think, Kolina. That's what all of this is about—to heal the schism. To show that it doesn't have to be the way it is. Two sides holding on to the past out of self-preservation."

She grunted.

Jori's hands rose. "Yes, there have been attacks, but hear me out. They are not a majority. Really. There are a lot of guys back at that mountain that just want peace and harmony, but also want to belong. That's why they ended up there in the first place. Ninety-nine percent of them would never say so, but I can feel it—see it when I talk to them. They're lonely."

"Whose fault is that?" she snapped, surprising herself.

He spread his hands. "If we are to make things better than preserving what is, we have to start somewhere."

"I know," she said, weary. "I know."

She nodded toward Odson's Shelby, pulling up to the curb outside the house they'd been surveilling.

"I hope this works," she said. "I still think you should accompany them."

"They'd recognize me, and I don't want to make the situation worse."

"Or fix it by example," she pointed out. "They know Odson. They know his stance on Aeleftherian relations."

"Maybe, but he's also established a relationship with the younger guys and is much more neutral."

They'd already been over the arguments as to who should go into the meeting and who shouldn't.

The last meeting had established that Odson's interests lay with the younger boys and getting them back to their families. Not politics, which is what Jori represented.

"I think this is exactly where you should be stepping in, Jori," she pressed. "You can relate, you have connections to Aeleftheria, you are of all three worlds."

She laughed, drawing his curious gaze.

"A few days ago, there is no way I would have ever even muttered words to those designs. I would have steered you far, far away from a group of potential recruits to strengthen your claim and your dragon militia. And here I am trying to shove you into the middle of it." She shook her head.

Jori chuckled. "It's Odson. He has that effect on people." He turned his attention back toward the house where the three men had gone inside. "Now that man, he would make a magnificent king. Between him and my dad, Jonathan—I just hope I can live up to their examples on how to be a good man."

Kolina didn't say anything as she considered this. She wanted to believe Jori was the person his words painted a picture of. But he was young by human standards; in his thirties. Still a child by dragon standards. Would his idealism go stale in a decade? Two? How would he view their hidden world a century from now?

Elora.

All his life, she'd been his guiding star, even when she wasn't there. If Kolina could trust anyone to be a positive influence in a realm of power such as a male dragon court, it was Elora.

Calm and graceful under any circumstance.

It was why Regina had chosen her to be her ambassador.

It was why she'd survived so long in captivity.

Why the male dragons had no notion of where the island was until weeks ago.

All because she loved her son so very deeply.

The irony was, that because she loved her son so much, and her people, she'd cryptically imparted details about Aeleftheria. He'd had no idea what he was really searching for when he'd crashed into it. But, it was her love that brought him, and indirectly the males, straight to Aeleftheria.

But it also resulted in felling Kargassa, one of their greatest enemies, and bringing Elora back to the world again.

And hopefully, back to Aeleftheria and to their queen, who missed her friend so very much.

"It's funny how things work out," she murmured.

"How do you mean?"

She shook her head. "Just how all of this has played out. Everything has its costs."

"I'm not sure what you mean specifically, but in general, yes. I agree."

CLIVE STOOD AT THE front of the rented room of the tiny community center in a hamlet outside of Charleston.

Surveying the group, he grunted. Not as many as he'd hoped, but still far more than just the two of them, the last time they'd attacked the island.

He glanced at the clock suspended on the wall at the back of the hall. He rolled his shoulders. Merwin hadn't joined them yet.

The young males, who had followed them from the camp outside of Black River, were clustered in the back. A bunch of other faces were now familiar, having joined along the way. Some of the ones he'd hoped would back them were absent.

The clock shuddered as the arms ticked across the hour mark.

Doesn't matter.

Merwin said he was working on a special weapon. Just had to give him a chance to get inside the queen's citadel.

"So, we're all here." One of the youngsters said. "What's the plan? Are we going to the island tonight?"

"Tomorrow night is the big night."

The door opened to reveal more attendees—the two faces he'd been hoping to see—arriving late, but arriving, nonetheless.

"Glad you could make it." He smiled.

They nodded and took up vacant seats.

Clive scowled as Odson followed them inside. "What the fuck are you doing here?"

"Forum said everyone was welcome."

"*You* are not."

Odson shrugged and sat on an empty plastic chair behind the other two newcomers.

One of the two late arrivals said, "You were saying tomorrow is the big night?"

"We'll fly out from a secluded section of the coastline."

"Not all of us fly, man."

Clive stared at him. The muscles in his chest tightened and heat crept up his neck. "You don't fly? Is there anyone else that doesn't fly?" He sneered.

Several hands went up.

"Fuck."

Hands on hips he turned away from the group, drawing several deep breaths through his nostrils. *Fuck. What now? Everything depended on an aerial attack.*

Where the hell is Merwin?

Fuck. Fuck. Fuck.

Think, Clive.

He turned back to the group. "Can you swim? If you can't swim, you'll just have to double up with someone else."

"You're kidding, right? I'm not fucking riding anybody."

"How else do you plan to keep up with us? You should have told me you didn't fly."

"You should have told us what the plan is."

"They're on an island. How else did you think we'd get there?"

The non-flyer's mouth snapped closed. He shrugged. "Boat? Or plane?"

Clive pinched the bridge of his nose.

His gaze swept the faces of the group, pausing on Odson's annoying smirk.

Handle this carefully, Clive. We need them to make this work.

Problem was, he and Merwin had always followed Stenlen's lead, who'd followed the king's orders.

Neither Clive—nor Merwin, as far as he knew—had planned a campaign before.

What now? New plan? Drop them?

"You don't find a way to be there without holding the rest of us back, you don't get your place on the island. You stay behind."

One of the younger kids from the camp spoke up. "You said we needed all the guys we could get."

"We need speed and stealth. That means flying high and attacking hard. We need enough guys to draw their guardians into battle so a small subset can infiltrate."

"You're going in after the queen," Odson said with a laugh. "You know she has a personal guard, right?"

"What the fuck do you know?" Clive challenged.

Odson stood up. "I know a lot more about the Aeleftherians than you do." He turned to look directly at the group of young males from the camp. "He's leading you all into a suicidal trap. Those guardians will kill you."

"We can handle ourselves."

"Ah, you can, huh? So, you're all trained in combat? Aerial tactics? I don't recall seeing a training field anywhere near the camp."

"Shut up Odson. They don't need to know any of that. They just have to distract them all long enough for Merwin to get inside."

"That kinda sounds like suicide to me" one of the late arrivals said. "And I have training."

Some of the other males watched the exchange with uncertain expressions.

"Get out," Clive said to Odson, "You're just here to stir shit up.

Odson ignored the order. "So you have someone infiltrating. To do what? Tie up the queen and her council and talk her into submission? You're an idiot."

Another surge of heat shot through Clive. "Fuck you, old man. You don't know a damned thing. You're just an old coward."

Odson chuckled, sauntering toward Clive. "Am I now?"

Clive's gaze flicked over the onlookers. No one else moved. Just watched the exchange with interest.

"I'm the coward intending to toss a handful of untrained youths at an island full of highly trained warriors as a distraction?"

"They're just females. We can take them." The young male insisted.

"You're idiots, too." Odson said to the youth. "Why do you think these two came here, banged up from battle, looking to recruit anyone stupid enough to join them?"

"Hey now," one of the other males objected.

"They got their asses handed to them by these harmless females; the ones that the lot of you think you're going to subdue long enough to take over their island? I don't give a shit about most of you. I'm just here to take those kids back there, home to their families."

"We don't want to go back."

Odson shrugged again. "I promised I'd try. No matter what. So if that means exposing this moron for what he is, then so be it."

The building haze of red encroached on Clive's vision. He snapped; with a raw snarl, his fist swung out like a boulder aimed for Odson's face.

There was no impact. Just the sensation of his arm being wrenched, his body spinning as his world turned upside down, and then the breath knocked from his chest as he hit the floor face first.

As soon as he could draw air back into his lungs, he stumbled to his feet.

Odson stood back several paces, calm, unconcerned.

"I've fought for many conquerors and warrior kings because I had nothing better to do with my long life. You're just as delusional as they were, only less intelligent," Odson said to Clive. To the rest of the room he said, "We are the apex species of this planet and should be able to control our baser urges for the benefit of our kind. And so long as there are morons like this guy around threatening those females, the division will remain. You'll have gained nothing but chest-thumping bragging rights of a conquest that no one will respect. Evolve."

Odson strode toward the door. Before he opened it, he turned back toward the young males. "I'll wait outside."

"Don't waste your time, Blackridge, we're not going back to the camp."

"You don't have to stay at the camp. But really, do you all hate females so much that you're willing to attack a whole tribe just to assert your independence? Your parents are probably at that camp to make life better for you—for everyone." He shrugged. "There are other tribes out there."

"Yeah, sure, like where?"

Odson's gaze flicked to Clive. "There's the mountain lair that Clive and Merwin were kicked out of. It has a new king; young, good head on his shoulders. There are tribes in the midwest, west coast, up north, down south, more overseas. You just have to ask. Things happen when we communicate with each other, and last longer than when we use our fists and claws." With that, he opened the door and left the hall.

"Finally. I thought he'd never shut up." Clive said to the group.

The younger males at the back were whispering among themselves.

"Odson Blackridge," one of the late arrivals said. "He's a legend."

"He's gone soft in his old age." Clive retorted.

"Yeah, well he's earned it. A millennium fighting. He's probably seen a thing or two."

A male standing against the wall to the left of the room picked up his jacket from the chair next to him. "I'm out of here. Good luck to y'all." He said with a nod to Clive and a glance around the room before he left.

Damn it.

"Yeah, me too. This big plan we've been waiting to hear doesn't sound like much of a plan at all." Another from the middle of the room rose from his chair and left the meeting.

Clive glanced at the clock again.

Where the fuck is Merwin?

Sweat trickled down the back of his neck. He struggled to remember the words he'd practiced before the meeting.

To the remainder of the group, he resumed his speech. "As I was saying, fly high, come in fast and draw the guardians away from the island. Merwin is working on something that will help secure the mission."

"Cool. Which is?" One of the guys prompted.

I'm losing them.

Another bead of sweat trickled from his temple. He scratched at it with his thumb, studying the clock again.

He said he'd be here.

Clive spun on his heel as the door opened. A gust of cool evening air swept into the room along with Merwin.

"You're late." Clive growled.

Merwin met his growl with a grin as he unslung his backpack from his shoulder, dropping it onto a nearby chair.

"Clive says you have a secret weapon of some kind."

"Sure do." Merwin said, unzipping the pack. Reaching inside, he withdrew a thin metal bracelet.

"Jewelry? Seriously?" Someone laughed. "You're kidding, right?"

Merwin shook his head, his grin widened. "Magically infused jewelry, my friend. It's spelled to bind power."

"Like Kargassa's collar." Clive breathed, excitement thrilling up and down his spine.

"Exactly." Merwin pointed at Clive.

"What collar?"

"Our late King Kargassa held in his collection of treasures one Aeleftherian ambassador, for a couple of decades with a collar similar to this bracelet. This is our long game."

The two late arrivals exchanged a glance.

"So, all we have to do is keep the guards busy long enough for you to get one of those on the queen? What about her personal guard, as Blackridge mentioned?"

"Clive spotted an entry when he moved in to destroy some of the village houses. There are several towers with platforms. And one stands taller than the rest—which I'm guessing is the queen's personal quarters. That's where I'll go in, while the guardians are drawn out."

"Say we're successful enough to shackle the queen? What stops the others from just killing the rest of us once the battle is over and done with? Rebellion."

Merwin lifted the pack. "This bag is full of shackles. We use the queen as leverage to get the guardians to stand down and submit. She will be vulnerable. They won't risk her life. We'll figure out which ones are threats and bind them too. The rest will fall in line." He flourished the bracelet through the air then let it drop to clatter against the others in the bag.

Clive watched their doubt turn to optimism.

He smiled.

We've got them!

Chapter 15

KOLINA SLID HER HIPS to the other side of the car seat, while keeping her attention on the community hall. She sat up straighter when Odson emerged from the building. He didn't turn toward them, but instead crossed the road to his car parked in the shadow of a massive tree. Leaning on the fender with arms crossed, he was clearly prepared to wait.

Minutes later, a man carrying a backpack on his shoulder sauntered up the street from the opposite direction, turned and entered the building. He didn't appear to have noticed Odson standing in the shadows across the road.

"That's Merwin," Jori murmured.

Her attention flicked back to Odson, who remained in place, looking for any who might see him like just another guy lurking in the darkness.

It was some time before the doors opened again, expelling males in singles and clusters. Odson ignored them all until the group of young males emerged.

The boy from the Black River jail, Ben's angry friend, was among them.

"Darren," Odson called out, drawing their attention toward his car.

With the car windows down and their sensitive hearing, their conversation was audible.

"Look, save your breath, we're not going back to the camp."

Odson shrugged. "I promised your folks I'd check in on you. And Ben misses you, so while I can't tell you what to do, I strongly suggest you at least text them to let them know you're okay."

"What, you're not going to talk us out of going to the island?"

"You're all what, sixteen? Seventeen? I may be ancient by your standards, but dragon memory is long and sharp. The world has changed since I was your age. A lot."

"What's your point?"

"My point is, that as old as I am, those two knuckleheads leading this little group of yours are spouting some pretty archaic ideology. If you want to be in with someone modern and relatable—and who has no interest in throwing you at some deadly claws for their own benefit—message me and I'll set you up with that new king I mentioned. The one that thinks. Like you should be doing."

Jori groaned.

Kolina chuckled.

"Yeah? You know where this *king* is?" Darren challenged.

"Darren. You know me. Have I ever fed you a line of bullshit? Yes, I know where he is. You heard what I said in there about fighting for kings and conquerors in my time. And this guy? He's actually going to do great things."

"How do you know him?"

Odson shrugged in his Odson way. "He's my nephew."

"Your nephew? Why aren't you king instead?"

Odson chuckled. "Being a king—a real king or queen is hard. It takes a special someone to do it right."

Jori sighed, hands rubbing over his face.

Kolina smiled at his discomfort. "He obviously has a great deal of respect and belief in you."

"Too much." Jori muttered.

Darren snorted. "And your nephew is that guy."

"Do you think Clive and Merwin are king material? Have you ever met a ruler?" Odson tapped his temple. "Think, guys. Aside from the adventure of seeking out an island and maybe battling some warriors. Think about what they're asking you to do. Without any training. Every soldier needs training. That's what boot camp is for."

"Does this king of yours train soldiers?"

"He has experienced warriors that handle that."

Darren and his friends laughed. "What, he doesn't do any of the fighting himself?"

"He's not looking to start a war with anyone at the moment." Odson dropped his hands to his hips. "Anyway, guys, I have things to do, so just text me if you're interested and we can talk some more."

"I want to meet this king." Darren challenged.

Kolina held her breath.

"Shit." Jori said. "This is risky."

"Mhmm." Kolina agreed. "You're not scared of a bunch of younglings, are you?"

"Nah. One of the things I learned from my dad, Jonathan, was that as part of a professor's first day of class was to enter the lecture hall like nothing intimidated you."

Kolina laughed. "Like you did when the queen summoned you to appear before the council."

Jori glanced at her with twinkling eyes. "Exactly. That was an incredibly intimidating display, by the way."

She tilted her head accepting his compliment. "I will inform the queen of your approval."

He chuckled, turning his attention back to Odson and the boys.

"He's traveling on business." Odson was saying. "New rule requires a lot of work. I can contact him to see if he can squeeze you in between appointments, once we fly out to meet him."

"New rule? What do you mean?" One of the other boys asked.

"New rule as in, just took over from the old king."

The boys looked at each other.

"What? Is he dead or something?"

"Awe, *Christ*." Jori muttered.

Odson nodded. "He was a real dick. The new king, Jori Mountainside, doesn't like anyone trying to control him. It didn't end well for the old king. As they say, the king is dead, long live the king." He shrugged.

"Holy shit!" one of them squeaked. "So he just mus-cled in and took over and everyone else let him? He must be scary as hell."

"What was the old king trying to make him do?" Darren demanded.

"King Kargassa wanted to use his son as a weapon against the Aeleftherians." Odson said.

Kolina chuckled softly. "Little did he know you couldn't fly."

Jori didn't answer the comment.

"So? Isn't that what Clive and Merwin are doing?"

"Yep. Look, I have to get going." Odson said, straight-ening.

"Wait. Why didn't he want to attack the Aeleftheri-ans? Is he scared?"

Odson chuckled. "There isn't much that guy is afraid of. No. His mother and his mate are Aeleftherian."

The boys exchanged looks.

"Yeah, imagine your father trying to force you to attack your mother or your girlfriend, just for trying to live their lives." Odson shrugged again and moved to get into the car this time. "Like I said, I have to go, guys. Message me if you're serious and I'll put in a word for you to see if he has a few minutes for you."

"Sounds to me like he's the kind of guy that would go after someone that tried to do that—attack the Aeleftherians."

"Smart kid." Jori murmured to Kolina.

She smiled.

Sitting inside the car, Odson closed the door and looked up at the boys. He tapped his temple. "Think about it. All of it. Text me when you're ready." He started the car, then looked up at them again. "Before it's too late." He drove off leaving the younglings to consider his warning.

"Seriously?" Darren scoffed.

"I'm inclined to agree." Jori mused.

"It was rather dramatic, wasn't it?" Kolina said.

"Hopefully effective."

"I don't know, Darren. He kinda makes sense," one of the boys said as they resumed walking up the street in Kolina and Jori's direction. Kolina scooted down in her seat so she would blend in with the shadows in the car.

Darren scoffed. "Nate, he's just trying to manipulate us. It's probably all a load of crap."

Kolina could practically hear the kid's eyes roll in his head.

The one called Nate said, "He seemed pretty chill to me. Besides, everyone back home always talks him up. And we all saw how fast he put Clive down when he took a swing at him."

The boys were almost in line with their car when Darren spun on his friend Nate. "Yeah? Well why don't you just run home like he says we should? Coward. You're no better than Ben."

"Hey, come'on, Nate isn't a coward and you know it, Darren. Neither is Ben, just because he's looking after his mom." The small group passed their car without noticing Kolina and Jori, too focused on their argument.

"A little pressure and you're both cracking already. We haven't even left yet."

"What about this new king?"

"What about him, Collin?"

"I think he sounds bad ass. It would be cool to see him for ourselves." Collin said.

Next to Kolina, Jori snorted again.

Their footsteps halted. "Look, we leave tomorrow night. We don't have time for you guys to flake out. Don't let Blackridge get to you. We're a new brotherhood, remember? We're forming something new. All in. This is a great opportunity. Clive said they'll have places in his court for us. What else do we have? There's nothing for us back home. I'm not going back. So, you're with me, or you're against all of us." Darren challenged his friends.

One of the others grumbled something, but they'd begun moving again, their voices growing faint.

"Well, that was interesting," Jori said as he started the car.

"Sounds like they're not *all* lost causes." Kolina said.

"Not yet." Jori navigated the car away from the curb and drove up the road, careful to turn their faces away from the males that were still emerging from the community center.

Kolina caught a glimpse of agent Carson Perenga and Bayn Long as they stepped outside with Clive and Merwin. "Whatever they're doing, I hope it works."

THEY REGROUPED AT A nearby diner and settled in to trade updates and plan.

Food orders placed, they all looked to Kolina.

"I wasn't anticipating leading an attack squadron when I left the island, but such is life, I suppose." She lifted a shoulder, her gaze sweeping the males present. "And certainly not with any of you in it."

"I spoke to Heidi Brandt while you were all out." Kymri said. "She sent word as you asked. It's hard to say how long it will take for the message to reach Aeleftheria."

Kolina nodded. "We've been on high alert since we got word the two of you were abducted.

Kymri hissed through her teeth. "They'll be exhausted. *Dragonsdammit.*

There was a pause in the conversation as the server returned with their drinks and cutlery.

"The best weapon we have is persuasion, and too little time to use it," Elora said once they were alone again.

"If all of the guys from Clive and Merwin's meetings show up, we're looking at about two dozen. And that's not accounting for anyone else on the forums that are hedging and waiting till the last minute to decide to back them."

"That's enough to cause a lot of destruction." Kolina said.

"And I'm almost useless in my state." Kymri said. "I can shift, but I can't hold it for long. I'm not even sure I can hold my dragon form long enough to make it all the way to Aeleftheria. I might be able to help bring one down in combat."

"You're not going into combat carrying my grandchild." Kolina said as Jori opened his mouth to protest the idea too.

"I'm aware I'd be a liability."

"We traveled by plane to get here, why don't we fly to Aeleftheria in a smaller plane? Like Elora's Cessna that Jori used to get there the first time." Jonathan offered.

Kolina's heart jumped in her chest. A human male traveling to Aeleftheria. Deliberately.

"No." Kymri snapped.

"But—." Jonathan tried again.

"Kymri, at least consider it." Jori soothed. "You handled flying here very well."

"They're unnatural." She insisted.

"They are." He agreed. "But sometimes necessary."

She blew out a breath, slumping.

The server returned with the first few plates, placing them on the table with a smile. Kolina returned it with thanks.

Kolina chuckled. "I haven't seen you behave like that since you were a youngling." She truly hadn't. Kymri was normally straight and unbending as a steel pole; her expressions masked.

Kymri straightened, her hand curled into a fist, and scowled at Kolina. A moment later, her features smoothed. Returned to those of the guardian commander that she was.

Kolina noted the smudges under Kymri's eyes.

She reached out, tentative, and rested her palm over her daughter's fist on the tabletop. "I know. It's the hormones. Can you think of a better option to get you to Aeleftheria before those males attack, now that we know it's happening tomorrow?"

Kymri studied Kolina's face for a long moment, then turned to Jonathan. "It is a good alternative. I will go with you."

Jonathan smiled.

Jori might not be the kindly Professor Jonathan Mountainside's biological son, but he certainly resembled Jonathan in his mannerism.

Before she'd left Aeleftheria, she'd instructed Zayli to report everything their senses picked up, including what they couldn't. What their instinct told them.

She looked to each face of the gathered. Kymri and Elora, Aeleftherians to their core.

And the males. Odson, Jori, Carson, Bayn and Jonathan.

We are not among enemies here.

No, *we are not.* Her dragon replied.

They were not as Clive and Merwin—Kargassa's followers—were.

No. Not all males sought to dominate.

They will fight with us.

Kolina looked at Jori.

He fought for Kymri, Elora and Aeleftheria.

He will fight for us.

What path would her son have taken, given the chance to live among the Aeleftherians?

What path has he taken?

We have not looked upon him since Kymri was born and presented to her sire as an infant. Her dragon mused.

Kolina drew in a long deep breath as her thoughts turned somber. Her eyes prickled.

Reaching for her glass, she sipped, keeping her gaze turned down, lest anyone should see the wave of raw emotion sweeping aside her steely exterior.

The others began eating their meals. She picked up her fork, picking at the food.

She had no idea how many other Aeleftherians returned to see their sons. It was a subject she never broached. Not wanting to invade their privacy. Not wanting to give away her own deeply buried secret. Not that she'd had a son, but that deeply buried secret of how much it had pained her to leave him to be raised by his sire.

To miss those moments, watching him grow and become a man.

By the time she'd given birth to Kymri, she'd buried those longings so deeply, it had distorted her ability to connect at the same level with her daughter. The one that had been acceptable—desired, to live among her sisters.

She glanced up at Jori.

What had Kymri's sire felt about the loss of his daughter? He hadn't seen her grow up either. Time stolen. She swallowed her emotions and drew deep breath.

"It is rare for Aeleftheria to allow males—of any species to visit the island. Let alone know the way." Kolina looked to Elora. "But times are changing and we must be open to the allies we have. The enemy already knows where we are."

"If we stop Clive and Merwin, the knowledge can still be guarded." Odson said.

Elora, still holding Kolina's gaze, nodded.

Kolina turned to Carson. "I assumed you were here on behalf of your agency. Do you plan to arrest these males? Because if they manage to make it anywhere near Aeleftheria, it will be a fight to the death. No quarter will be given."

The agent nodded. "If I can bring them in, I will. When Bayn and I headed this way, I was investigating their forum, like a terrorist cell, which is what they are. But I'm going to help protect Aeleftheria. We all are." He nodded to Bayn and the others.

Bayn leaned forward on his chair, phone in hand. "Forum activity is heating up. Looks like more dragons are coming now that there is a definite launch time."

Kolina's heart sank into her stomach.

How can we stop them?

Chapter 16

"I HATE THIS—THIS FEELING of uselessness." Kymri muttered.

Jori pulled her into his arms. "I know."

They stood in the hangar of a small airport waiting for technicians to finalize their work before releasing their charter.

She sank into him. "This is exactly what I've trained my whole life for. What I'm made for. And now the time is here..."

Jori squeezed her tighter.

"I can't believe my mother is on board with allowing your father to fly to the island with me, let alone work with all of you. It's...bizarre to see her so cooperative."

His chest rumbled against her ear as he chuckled. "People change."

"Not my mother. She's unrecognizable."

"Maybe leaving the island for a little while has done her some good."

"Maybe."

"Or Odson. He has a way of getting under people's skin."

"I bet Heidi Brandt softened her up first. She got to me too, when we met."

"Or," Jori leaned back so he could look down into her face. "It was you. You and that little dragon baby in your belly."

"It feels like a rock with that protective barrier it—."

"She."

"She. Or he. Created to protect it—himself from my magic when I shift."

"Do you think she'll be a metal dragon like you, or an earth dragon like me? I still can't believe I'm a frikking dragon, Kymri."

Kymri shrugged. "Maybe a bit of both? Hopefully, he'll inherit your heart, and my flight skills." Her mouth snapped closed.

If we survive this invasion.

Jori frowned as he studied her face. "It's okay, we'll find a way to get through this."

"If those males make it to the archipelago, nothing will be the same. From what my mother said about the last attack, it looks like they're out to break us or destroy us."

"And I don't know how many of the guys at the mountain I can trust yet. It's tempting to call them in but I can't risk them turning."

"And leading them straight to Aeleftheria, along with Clive and Merwin."

Jori nodded. "And even with what you've been teaching me about flight and dragon fighting tactics, I don't know how much use I'll be tomorrow. All I've got is my size."

"And your right to the tribe's throne by acknowledgment of the previous king. That is something powerful."

Jori snorted. "A lot of those guys see me as a usurper. And I can barely *dragon*. I'm a joke."

"You're not and never will be a joke, Jori. We just have to speed up your *dragoning* timeline so that they will know how formidable you are."

He looked up over her head. "Dad is coming." He dropped his gaze back to her face, caressing her with his eyes before lowering his lips to hers.

She clung to him, like she never had anyone else in her life. Her lifeline. The father of her child. Her mate.

She savored the sensation of his lips on hers, while enveloped in his strong, comforting arms.

When the kiss ended and she looked into his face, she reached up to stroke his bearded cheek. "You, are a *king*."

"Kymri, the plane is ready for us." Jonathan Mountainside's soft voice pulled her attention from her beloved.

Jori smiled down into her face, taking up her hands in his, kissing each. "This is the very airport I left from the day our worlds collided. My dad is a good pilot. You're in good hands, so try not to panic." He grinned with a twinkle in his eyes.

She snorted, pulling away. "I never panic."

He squeezed her hands, then released her.

"Kymri," Kolina's voice sounded from behind her.

With her eyes on Jori's, she drew a breath, released it, then turned to face her mother.

This could all end in disaster.

She stared at her mother's face with new eyes.

Kolina had changed in the weeks since they'd last seen one another.

That wasn't quite right.

She recalled the day she'd awakened in the infirmary when she'd collapsed after a few hours of guardian duty.

The day she'd learned she was with child. She awakened to her mother's face alight with delight. Which she'd never seen before.

This spark of life in her womb had given something to her mother, as well as to herself and Jori.

It was that moment, she'd begun to see her mother in a different light. And the transformation in the weeks since then was... She couldn't find the words as she looked into her mother's eyes.

There'd always been a distance between them. The threads that linked them, growing taut and strained over the course of her lifetime.

Kolina stepped toward her and Kymri *felt* her presence.

"We have so much to talk about when this is over. I have much to tell you that I have kept locked away for so very long."

Kymri's breath caught at the unexpected words and the vulnerable expression in Kolina's eyes as she swallowed, looking as though she struggled not to take back the words.

Kolina cleared her throat. "Elora has reached out to allied tribes that she had connections to before she was lost to Aeleftheria."

"Will they come?"

Kolina shrugged. "She doesn't know for certain." Her eyes dropped to Kymri's belly. Her fingers twitched as she looked up again. "When your child is born, would you like to present him or her to your sire, if he still lives?"

Kymri's heart stopped.

Searing cold swept her body driving the breath from her lungs before the sensation was replaced by a wave of heated emotion. She blinked. "M-My sire? You've never spoken of him before. W-why now?"

Kolina shrugged, her gaze returning to Kymri's belly, refusing to meet her eyes. "Things will be different for you. You will make different choices from what I did." She finally met Kymri's gaze. "If things look as though the island won't make it, I want you to flee, along with the others with children." She hesitated on a breath, considering her next words. "I may not make it out of this. So if I don't, you should know that your sire and your brother were in the far-east, living among a clan of tiger shifters."

Kymri's head spun. Shock rippled through her.

Brother?

"Mother..." What could she say? This was too much all at once. "I have a brother?"

Kolina's head jerked in a sharp nod.

"I won't flee," Kymri said, "Guardians fight."

"You will. This time. You are not a guardian anymore. You know the protocols."

She did.

She also knew that Kolina would fight to the death to protect their queen and their people. It was what Kymri was trained to do. But she carried a child now. And the

Aeleftherian children's lives were as valuable and sacred as their queen's.

We do not protect ourselves by fleeing, we protect Aeleftheria's future.

Her dragon reminded her.

"Go, give us the time we need," Kolina said, stepping back and away from Kymri.

The withdrawal of Kolina's presence was sharp. The familiarity of their distance returned to fill the void.

This was all she would get of her mother, after all this time, when their relationship had finally made a new turn.

Unless they survived.

She nodded and backed away. "We will talk when this is done." She turned toward Jonathan Mountainside, who waited for her. She met Jori's eyes.

I love you.

He smiled, but worry for her safety clouded his eyes.

Straightening her spine, she followed her mate's father to the metal contraption she dreaded being trapped inside.

Dragons were meant to fly with their own wings. Not rely on fragile human inventions.

She sent a prayer up to the dragon goddess that this plane would not end up mangled like Jori's had on entering the magnetic and magical fields of the Bermuda Triangle that protected Aeleftheria.

KOLINA STOOD RIGID, WATCHING Kymri depart.

Her heart still hammered like beating wings in her chest, making every nerve in her body raw.

She heard Elora's approach before she spoke.

"It's good you finally told her."

"I didn't know how." She swallowed the surge of heartache that reared up into her throat.

"I know." Elora's touch was feather-lite, almost imperceptible. "Jonathan is a good pilot. With Kymri's guidance when the instruments fail, he can land them safely.

Kolina nodded.

She turned to Elora. "I don't know if we can stop them. Are you sure you want to do this, Ambassador? You've only just returned to your family."

Elora glanced at the door her beloved had just left through, then back to Kolina.

"I'm sure. We all are." She reached for Kolina's hand. "Our children are bonded. That makes us family. More than just Aeleftherians."

Emotion surged through Kolina. She blinked, looking over Elora's shoulder to where Odson and the others stood, conversing.

Too *much.*

Too much emotion in the last few days.

She gave herself a little shake, dislodging the discomfort.

The corners of Elora's lips tilted upward with a knowing smile. She leaned toward Kolina and whispered. "Your secret is safe, Steelscale."

Kolina laughed. "You've been missed, my friend. The queen will be happy to see you again."

"She will be very cross I abandoned her and Aeleftheria for my family."

"Mmm. I think she's more understanding than you remember her to be. Perhaps your absence shook something in her."

"Perhaps." Elora's expression turned thoughtful as she turned to gaze on her son. "I'm sorry our actions led to the exposure of Aeleftheria. But I will never regret the choice to stay with him." She turned back to Kolina again. "I wish you could have had those years too. Like I did." The depth of her empathy was clear in her eyes.

"We have to prepare," Kolina said, voice soft.

The sound of the small plane's engine vibrated through the hangar.

Moving toward the window, they all waited and watched as it taxied, paused for further checks, then geared up and took off. As soon as it was out of sight, everyone left to regroup.

As soon as night fell, they had work to do.

Chapter 17

Merwin surveilled the skies.

Five revolutions of guardian patrol.

He squinted. His keen dragon sight narrowed on the three even dots marring the clear blue sky.

Soon, this would be his section of sky.

He'd flown out, after the meeting, in the late hours of the night. In the end, he'd decided to go it alone rather than risk detection.

Flying as high as the atmosphere would allow, he watched, alert to their location. By pure luck, he'd managed to penetrate their territory between patrol sweeps, which he noted had doubled.

As soon as the tail of the archipelago came into view, he swept the skies again for those telltale dots in the darkness.

His chest tightened. There they were.

The wind pushed their scent toward him.

Inhaling deeply, he savored their unique flavors twined together by the twist of the breeze.

Soon. Soon we will own you—all of you.

He dove.

Drawing a deep breath as he angled his head downward, his snout broke the surface and he plunged deep into the darkness of the ocean at a precise angle so as not to cause a massive splash, and sank straight to the ocean floor.

He waited for as long as his lungs could hold, which, in his dragon form was a long, long time. And still he waited until his chest burned.

When his lungs threatened to open of their own volition, he pushed for the surface, only allowing his head to rise and draw air.

In the distance the guardian patrol grew smaller.

He remained undetected.

Drawing another deep breath, he swam toward the nearest island.

A dull white shape glowed under the moonlight. Gaining the shoreline, he approached it to discover that it was an over-turned, wingless plane. There was nothing else nearby, other than a scattered pile of charred wood from a long-abandoned campfire.

He glanced at the backpack he'd carried looped around a claw and had cradled in his paw as he flew. He shifted to human form.

No other indications of a camp. The interior of the plane was devoid of any other equipment or clues to a survivor.

I can use this.

He climbed into the body of the broken plane, hauling his backpack. There he withdrew some clothes, a bottle of water and a protein bar and set them aside while he dressed. He wasn't very hungry yet, as he'd gulped up some fish while he swam.

As he pulled his shirt over his head, his ears strained. Listening through the rush of ocean waves on the island shore, and the wind rustling the nearby trees. He could not detect the sound of air rushing around dragon wings.

But he wouldn't let his guard down. No time to become sloppy, like they had in the past. They had a plan this time, and he was going to stick to it.

Kolina's hands curled into fists at her sides as she watched the males pace the hotel room. She stood next to the bed, where her backpack rested, feet spread to shoulder width, and moved her hands behind her back. The edges of the locket which bore the insignia of her people and denoted her rank bit into her palm, gripped inside her fist.

Outside the hotel room, the sky darkened.

Next to the door, Odson check his phone again.

Her fingers tightened on the object further as Jori passed back and forth between Odson and herself.

Elora's son and brother; her husband en route with Kymri. All fighting to protect Aeleftheria.

When this is finished. I will find my son.

And pray to the dragongoddess that he forgives me. And if he doesn't, then I will have tried and maybe Kymri can connect with him and their sire.

Their father.

Kolina sighed, moving the locket from one hand to the other.

Her gaze slid to Elora, who sat on the bed, watching her. She smiled.

"I never would have dreamed such a thing, but I'll wager you did." Kolina said to Elora.

Elora inclined her head. "I had hopes that one day we could work together."

Kolina stepped around the end of the bed into the space between the two, closer to Elora, and sat on the edge, facing her.

"You *will* come back with me?" When Kolina set foot in Black River, it was not a question. She was no longer certain of things anymore.

"I will. I intend to do my part to change things on Aeleftheria. I always intended to."

"Just had a twenty-year detour getting home."

Elora laughed, making light of the imprisonment she'd endured. "Yes. A detour." Her gaze fell to her son, her expression softened. "My report to Regina will be extensive. There is much to catch up on."

"But you won't stay."

Elora's gaze slid back to Kolina. Her smile faded as sadness touched her lips. "He will need me—*they* will need me."

"I don't know how you can stand remaining in a mountain lair where you were held captive for so long, Elora." Kolina blurted.

She shrugged. "I don't love the idea, and I do avoid certain areas of the place. But Jori is determined to make it something new. Something better."

"I'd have set it ablaze."

"I think he considered it. But if he had, those males that remained would have nowhere to live."

Kolina snorted. "Compassion is not one of my strengths."

Elora shrugged. "Change needs something it can get a claw into in order to move forward."

Kolina sighed. "I know." She flipped the locket over in her hand. "I know Kymri won't return to Aeleftheria. At least not to stay. I see that, as much as I wish I didn't. I can't ignore it."

"Regina won't be pleased to lose another talented guardian commander."

"No, she won't. But, I think she will understand. Especially with you there to advocate for Jori and the mountain tribe."

"I hope so."

"Hope." Kolina tested the word on her tongue. She blew out her breath. "We need more allies."

"Friends. We need more friends."

Kolina looked up into Elora's stoic face and nodded. "You were able to connect with them? Our *friends*?"

"Yes."

"Will they come?"

Elora shrugged. "The relationship went stale after I went into the mountain. I don't know. But I have hope."

"They're on the move," Odson said, "Bayn texted a location. The group is gathering on the beach."

Jori stopped pacing to grab his jacket and keys from the small table.

Elora stood, smoothing out her clothing.

Kolina gripped the locket in her hand.

Should I give it to Jori, for Kymri, in case I don't make it out of this?

"I need a minute," she said reaching for the hotel notepad and pen to print a name and place in tiny letters. Tearing the small portion of paper away, she rolled it tight and slipped it into her locket next to the curl of soft black hair. She looked up.

The others waited by the door for her.

"If something happens to me, ensure Kymri receives this." She held up the locket before securing it into a zipped pocket of her backpack, which she slung over her shoulder to deposit in the trunk of Odson's Shelby.

They drove to where Bayn's message said the gathering was happening. Elora rode with Jori, following Odson's car.

Kolina glanced at Odson's tense expression as he drove. "I don't know how Elora does it. She has hope." She was a compressed coil waiting to spring.

"Hope for the best, expect the worse."

Kolina snorted. "She didn't mention the second part."

"She's too diplomatic for that."

She nodded. "Even if we can't talk them out of it—which I think is a waste of time to even bother trying—we can disable a few and give Aeleftheria a better chance to defend herself."

"Clive's eye hasn't healed," he said, glancing at the GPS on his phone clipped to the dashboard.

"Good. Then I'll make it my mission to take the other."

"Cold."

"Pragmatic."

"I approve."

She laughed. "So you haven't gone completely soft after all."

"Not completely." He grinned. "Just where younglings and puppies are involved."

A fraction of the pre-battle tension eased.

"I'm glad you finally seem to be trusting me. Trusting us."

"I haven't much choice."

It was Odson's turn to snort.

"No, you're right," she said, "I'm going soft too—where younglings are concerned."

The scent of the ocean grew stronger as the highway edged closer to the coast. They were almost there.

"I overheard what you said to Kymri. About your son. Not that it's my business, but if you want to see him, you should try."

"And if he doesn't want to see me?"

"Then you'll know."

"Expect the worst, hope for the best?"

"Something like that."

The GPS indicated they'd arrived at a dirt turn-off that led to the coast. They would leave the cars there and walk the rest of the distance.

Kolina stood next to Odson's car. The moon hung suspended over the ocean waves rolling toward them. The wind and the crash of those waves was all she could hear. The scent of the water, beach scrub, and seaweed filled her nostrils, reminding her of home.

Had Kymri and Professor Mountainside made it to the queen?

Of course they had. She squeezed the doubt out of her mind as she pictured the battered body of Jori's Cessna abandoned on the tail island of their archipelago.

He'd only survived because Kymri had made sure of it, cushioning the plummet toward the ocean and pushed what was left of the plane out of the water toward land.

Kymri wouldn't fail in this, even if their little plane did.

Voice somber, Jori said, "Let's go."

The four of them looked at each other, preparing to confront the growing threat.

The sound of more cars pulling up to their location drew their attention.

Engines cut and five figures exited the SUV.

Odson grinned.

Kolina recognized Ben and his mother, and the young man belonging to the pregnant Aeleftherian. The others were unknown.

Odson strode forward to greet them.

Kolina, Jori and Elora followed, making introductions.

Ben, his mother Allison, her partner Emma, Darren's father Jason, and the young man, Mark.

She stared at the collection of newcomers, trying to figure them into potential battle tactics. Jason and Emma were human. Mark was a bear shifter. Though Ben and Allison were dragons, they were inexperienced.

But their number had just doubled.

Kolina felt Elora's eyes on her face.

"I can hear your mind running through battle tactics Kolina." Elora said. "Diplomacy first."

"Right."

Talking.

Trust.

Another car pulled up alongside the others.

She almost laughed as their little band grew again.

Who else would come to a face off with a couple dozen male dragons?

She glanced at Jason and Emma. What could these two humans possibly do? Even Mark, as a bear shifter, was little match for a dragon.

Another car arrived, and then another.

Giddiness rippled through Kolina's gut.

On the outside, she remained impassive. Assessing.

Chapter 18

A DISTANT WHINE PULLED Merwin's attention to the western sky.

Squinting, he honed in on a whitish dot moving unsteadily in his direction. The direction of Aeleftheria's archipelago.

It sounded as though the engine struggled to hold on, cutting out and gasping.

It grew larger as it grew louder.

A small plane, here, in the middle of the Bermuda triangle. Headed straight for Aeleftheria.

Coincidence?

It didn't matter. The thing was making noise that could draw the attention of the guardians if it hadn't already. He'd been monitoring their patrol schedule, and he was sure the arrival of this little aircraft was right in the middle of two rotations.

He had to act fast.

Kill the noise before it was noticed and drew attention to this area, where he lurked.

He was about to shift to intercept it when the engine coughed, the plane bounced on an air current and the propellers stopped turning. It hobbled through the air like a bumblebee unsure which way to go first when approaching a garden of bright flowers to land on.

Finally, it chose this one.

With the engine dead, the only sound was of the wind whistling around the wings and body. It hit the water with a hard splash and a crack as parts crumpled under the direct impact.

Merwin observed, curious.

Would the occupants survive?

Shielding his eyes, he turned to the north, watching, then the south, waiting.

No patrol yet.

Two figures emerged from the downed plane as it listed in the water and began to sink. They called to one another over the waves.

Impassive, almost bored, Merwin watched.

The plane disappeared under the water. The survivors bobbed and rode the waves as the ocean carried them toward the shore of his island.

He could feed his dragon and no one would ever know they were here. Just two more travelers lost to the mystery of the Bermuda Triangle.

No one had to know.

He sniffed.

The faint scent of female dragon tickled his nostrils. He looked up again. Nothing else in the sky.

His eyes narrowed on the two, nearly to the beach now.

He laughed into the wind, the sound carried away, weaving between the palm trees then dispersed across the island.

A female dragon and a human.

Her scent was now familiar.

Mountainside's woman.

This was just too fucking funny.

What was her name? Steelscale? Kymri Steelscale.

He watched from the shade of a palm tree at his back, arms crossed. His backpack, full of the spelled bracelets, rope, duct tape and zip-ties, among other things, rested at his feet. He reached down and pulled two bracelets from his pack and tucked them into his pocket.

They were indeed bound for Aeleftheria. Probably to warn them of the attack.

He'd been tense, unsure if the spelled bracelets would work, but this happy coincidence was the perfect opportunity to test them out.

She was almost as valuable as the queen herself; through her, he could control the usurper. Kargassa had made mistakes. Merwin wouldn't.

She was pregnant, weakened and vulnerable.

Her companion was a useless human.

Too easy.

As they stumbled onto the beach after their lengthy fight with the ocean to reach the sand, he stepped out of the shadows and into searing sunlight. "Well isn't this a welcome surprise, Steelscale."

Eyes wide, she shouted to her companion, "Jonathan, get away!"

The older man turned to her, then saw what she looked at with such alarm, but he didn't run as she'd ordered.

Her hands clenched and the air around her wavered as she tried to shift.

Merwin chuckled. "Having some troubles over there? Looks like you can't seem to find your dragon?"

"Screw you, Merwin," she spit, still trying to shift.

"Maybe later, love. I have plans tonight. Afterward? I think a little three-way with the queen would be perfect."

Her energy rippled, obscuring the silhouette of her human form, but it wasn't strong enough. She stumbled with the effort and subsequent failure.

The man called Jonathan moved to her side. There was nowhere for them to go.

But that didn't mean Merwin had all day to toy with them.

A glance out to sea confirmed the completion of the plane's disappearance under the water.

They could still alert the patrols.

He moved toward them and their stances turned defensive.

With one blow, he knocked the man to the ground. He struggled to rise, but couldn't.

She screamed his name, but turned on Merwin with glittering steel in her eyes. She couldn't shift, but her dragon was close to the surface and would be a little more challenging to subdue than the human.

"I don't have time for this shit, bitch." He snarled and swung a fist in her direction.

She dodged and hit him twice with quick strikes.

He stumbled back and shook his head.

Her fists were coated with metallic scales. She shook out her hands, razor sharp claws extended from her fingers. She looked as though she wore gauntlets.

Normally he would enjoy the challenge of a good fight. But right now, he needed to get her out of view before the next patrol flew by.

Without killing her.

She put up a fight, but ultimately, his weight and strength overcame her. Barely.

He'd pinned her face down in the sand, arm wrenched behind her. With his knee in her back as he fumbled to extract one of the bracelets from his pocket, mumbling the words to activate the spell.

He locked it in place. The bracelet's magic reacted to her dragon magic, sparking and sizzling, forcing her scales and claws to recede, leaving her completely human.

He flipped her over and drove his fist into her cheek, knocking her unconscious.

By then the older man had got to his feet and threw himself at Merwin to stop him from hitting her. Another hit and he was out cold next to her.

It took a few more minutes to grab his pack of subjugation supplies, bind and drag them to the original abandoned plane nearby. Shoving them both inside, he sought a palm branch to brush the beach clean of their tracks and returned to the shadows of the palm trees which sheltered him from any overhead view.

After a few minutes, his pulse returned to normal and he risked peeking out.

Three dark specs appeared.

I can't be discovered yet. It's too early.

He still had to wait for Clive and the other guys to arrive and provide the distraction he needed.

For now, he would be occupied with keeping his hostages quiet and the guardians ignorant of their presence.

He crouched in the shadow of the tree, keeping his profile and scent as close to the earth as possible.

Watching. Waiting for the right time.

ZAYLI NARROWED HER EYES, straining to see further on the horizon.

She blinked.

What was that?

She thought she had seen a dark shape drop toward the surface of the water in the far distance. Testing the air, she scented only her companions, the ocean and vegetation from nearby islands behind her patrol squad. The wind blew from behind them, anything ahead would be pushed away. As their flight arc drew closer to the place where she saw the movement, she angled downward, gliding closer to the water, searching.

Unable to detect a scent, or shapes in the water, she swooped lower, her gut tight.

Her companions cast her sidelong glances as they followed her lead.

Her senses detected nothing out of the ordinary.

Discomfort gnawed at her gut.

She growled, gliding lower, almost skimming the surface of the water before pulling up again. Maintaining a height of about one hundred feet from the surface, she angled toward the tail of the island chain. High enough for optimal view, low enough to detect changes on the island's face.

No signs of occupation. The overturned plane remained as it had been for weeks since Jori Mountainside had crashed it there, throwing everyone's lives into turmoil.

They'd received word from the continent that Kolina and Odson Blackridge were pursuing the males and that the threat was growing.

Continued vigilance was necessary.

The squad fanned out, circling the area again, unable to see, scent or hear an intruder despite their keen dragon senses.

She blew out a breath. Too many long hours of patrolling were starting to get to her. She needed to rest. They all needed to rest, but until they had further confirmation one way or another from Kolina, they couldn't let their guard down.

They resumed their normal route back to the main island, where she would make her full report. She would also make a verbal report to Launia about the unease in her gut.

Clive strutted before the gathered group, as was his new routine.

I'm a king now.

He'd decided that morning to use affirmative language.

He no longer thought *When I'm king...*

He decided.

He had a tribe prepared to follow him to their new domain.

He had his closest buddy, Merwin, working to secure his queen.

Therefore, he was a king.

Two dozen males had checked in at the meeting point. More were expected.

They arrived in spurts, like they had for the general meetings. Mostly the same faces that had followed from town to town.

He smiled. More faces he didn't recognize. He nodded, acknowledging the newcomers.

The wind rolled in with the ocean waves, buffeting his back as he waited.

He breathed deeply of the fresh air as it whipped past, ensuring the scents of so many male dragons were carried away inland.

Behind him the moon rose higher over the water, illuminating the beach.

"Almost everyone is here, Clive," one of the younger guys said. David? Darren? Yes, Darren. His friends stood off to the side looking sullen, not making much effort to interact with the rest of the group.

He faced the center of the gathered, cleared his throat, and spoke loudly so that his voice would carry above the crashing waves and strong wind.

"Welcome everyone. Welcome to the big night. Tonight we take our rightful place among the Aeleftherians and begin something new. A new tribe of integrated dragons. We have a bright future ahead of us."

He ensured he had their full attention before continuing. "We have a male awaiting our arrival. He has a plan to infiltrate and secure the queen and her council. All we have to do is draw out their guards and keep them busy. Expect them to put up a fight, but try not to kill any of them unless you absolutely have to. As I'm sure you're aware, we'll need them for breeding to secure our population—our future. There are a lot of us, so the whole operation shouldn't take long to subdue them."

He rubbed his hands together, pacing again as he looked over his male fleet.

"As I mentioned before. Those of you that can't fly will have to find a way to follow us without slowing us down. We're going in high and will dive hard. Contain and control."

"Who's that?" someone asked, looking up the beach.

He turned to see who approached. He frowned, squinting into the distance. A clump of shapes moved toward them. He squinted harder with his good eye.

Where those female shapes among them? That couldn't be right. Who were they?

A sense of familiarity tickled his nape before his keen dragon sight came into focus.

Fuck.

Kargassa's Aeleftherian ambassador pet, the usurper heir, Mountainside, and Blackridge headed the approaching group. More faces came into view. Some he recognized from the camp and Black River. Many others he'd never seen before.

"What's this?" one of his men asked. "More recruits? With females?"

"Just a slight delay."

Murmuring rippled through his gathered.

The Ambassador's gaze was locked on Clive's face.

Clive glanced from her to his group.

I'm not going to let them try to stop me. We waited too long for this. Too, dragonsdammed, long.

His gaze flicked back and forth between the two groups.

Think.

Merwin wasn't here to help. What would Stenlen have done? He was always the quick thinker. It was why he had been their squad leader. The traitor.

He was so busy trying to think, he hadn't heard what was being said.

He blinked.

The Aeleftherian ambassador was addressing his fleet. Greeting them...like a politician.

His gaze swept their confused expressions, some returned her greeting.

No. No, no, no!

"You won't talk us out of this mission. You have no
right to the king's throne. Usurper. Murderer!" he spat
at Mountainside as he panicked for something righteous
to say that would shore up the support of his gathered
males.

Mountainside narrowed his attention on Clive, approaching him. Odson Blackridge moved in a step behind
him, as they broke away from their group.

All he said was, "Go home. All of you. Just go home.
There will be no Aeleftherian conquest."

The wind shifted, circling around the two groups.

Clive laughed.

They weren't all dragons. There were other shifters
among them. And humans! Humans!

"You can't stop us."

Mountainside shrugged.

Heat flared through Clive's body. His hands curled into
fists. He glanced at Blackridge, remembering the last
time he'd taken a swing, and decided calm and steady was
the best approach.

*We're wasting time. They're not going to attack us.
They're just posturing with these extra...people.*

Two more figures appeared from the darkness. The
two that always seemed to show up late to every meeting.

Still. They were here, shoring up his odds even more.

To his new tribe he said, "Ignore them. Let's go."

Chapter 19

Kolina observed Clive.

His eye was indeed useless. Scarred from her back claw during their underwater scuffle.

Her muscles itched for battle.

I hate talking.

She strode right up to him and looked him straight in the eye.

"How's the eye, Clive? Doesn't look like it's healing so well."

His face darkened several shades as he scowled at her. "You." He spit. "You're the bitch that did this to me."

"I did." She smirked.

In her peripheral, she caught the tightening of his hand.

He wants to hit me.

She smiled now. "I wonder how long it will take me to put out the other eye?"

He seethed.

Odson stepped between them.

"I thought you went home," Darren said, stepping forward. "We told you we don't want you here."

"You said you wanted to meet the new king. So, meet the new king." He turned on Darren.

Darren straightened, mouth snapping shut as his eyes swiveled from Odson to Jori then to Clive and back to Jori, then dropping open again.

Kolina almost laughed.

Darren and his young friends stepped closer, staring at the new king with his hair tied in a sloppy man-bun, AC/DC t-shirt, cargo shorts and Timberland boots. His exposed arms and legs displayed a colorful collection of tattoos, most of which were abstract images of Aeleftheria. From their meeting in the Aeleftherian council chamber, she knew his chest and back were also covered.

"I've seen you." Darren squinted at Jori. "You have a Vlog. You're that guy that goes around the world documenting adventures. You disappeared just off the coast here." Darren's eyes flicked back and forth between Jori and Kolina and Odson.

"I did." Jori said.

"Dude, that show rocks!" One of the other younglings exploded. "I subscribe to your channel! Man, I can't believe you're here! Here! And you're one of us? What the hell, man?"

Agent Perenga and Bayn approached from behind Clive's gathered males.

"You're late!" Clive barked.

Bayn shrugged. "Traffic."

Carson moved forward with a grin, "Hey man, good to see you." He reached out to grasp Jori's hand and gave him a fist bump.

Kolina's attention whipped back to Clive's face as his expression crumbled into even darker shades of puce.

If he were human, she might have been concerned he'd pop a blood vessel.

Might have. But she generally didn't concern herself with humans, and Clive needed to be brought down anyway.

His head turned toward his followers.

She swept them too.

Half looked bewildered by the turn of events. The other half looked ready to attack this new obstacle. Those were the ones that were all in with Clive.

"Darren, I've come to take you home," Jason said, stepping out of the small crowd behind them, exposing himself to the growing tension between the dragonkind.

"Dad?" Darren gaped, his head turned toward Ben as he appeared next to Jason. Darren looked at the others from the camp. Tears appeared in his eyes, but his face solidified his determination. He shook his head and backed away.

"Who are all these people?" another youngling asked.

"Friends and allies." Elora said. "This is what I do. It's what I did before Clive's former king, Kargassa, imprisoned me. I was forming partnerships with other shifter and paranormal communities on behalf of my Aeleftherian queen." She turned to Clive. "And now, I work for King Mountainside, rightful heir to the Mountain tribe."

"He murdered my king." Clive spat.

"Your king tried to force his will by threatening my life and that of his mate. Is that traditional dragon practice? To kill the king's consort and heir's mate? And I recall how you held a blade to our throats, Clive," she challenged him, then looked to the others. "Is that what you're all looking for? A rule of brutality? Following Clive will lead you to nothing but constant conflict. Even if you were to conquer Aeleftheria, you would never know peace, because we would find every way we could to free ourselves, including slay you in your sleep to do it."

Kolina stared at Elora. Diplomacy at its hardest.

Clive sprang for Elora's throat.

Kolina darted between them. Drawing on her dragon power, scales covered her arm as she brought her elbow up to connect with his nose. It crunched. His blood blotted her shirt as she sank into a crouch, ready for his next move.

Around her chaos erupted as Clive's followers moved to back him and everyone else moved to stop them.

She pushed Elora behind her, intending to protect her with the same ferocity she would the queen. As an Aeleftherian ambassador, she *was* the queen off Aeleftherian soil. It didn't matter if she also chose to serve Jori.

She launched herself forward, striking Clive multiple times before he shook off the shock of her first strike. She aimed for his good eye, but he dodged, allowing the blows to land on other spots on his head.

From the corner of her eye, some of the other shifters appeared to surround Elora. She was a dragon and could do much more damage than they could in her shifted form.

It was a show of solidarity.

With a sweeping glance, she took in the scene. "You're not as united as you thought, Clive. Your younglings appear to have switched sides and a few others have abandoned you."

"Not all of them," he growled, and shifted.

The force of the magic from his shift sent her flying backwards. She caught herself, landing on her feet, then ran toward him while launching into her own dragon and collided with him, setting him off balance, tearing at him as he stumbled.

He roared in her face.

Her jaws snapped at his snout while her claws extended for his unscarred eye, trying to finish what she started. She would do everything she could to end his terrorizing of her people.

He got a hind foot up between them and kicked her hard, throwing her back toward where their non-dragon allies fought.

Her wings snapped out, catching herself before she crushed them with her mass. She flapped, twisting her body in a clean arc, and dove for his throat, harrying the much larger aggressor.

Following Clive's lead, several others shifted and launched into the air.

Odson soared over Kolina's head, knocking two of the shifted males out over the ocean, pushing the fight away from land and away from the dense city population nearby.

Clive roared again, calling to his males, leading them toward Aeleftheria.

The shifters and humans left behind couldn't stop the dragons, but they did what they could to slow them down by keeping them engaged.

She flapped, holding her position to monitor Elora's situation as she caught her breath before she went after Clive again.

Below, agent Carson Perenga ran toward the ocean, diving and shifting. His dark form moved below the surface as fast as she could fly, and as a metal dragon, she was one of the fastest. A moment later, he erupted from the ocean, mightier than an Orca reaching for airborne prey. His jaws closed on the foot of one of the dragons engaged with Odson and dragged him down below the surface, twisting and sinking.

Bayn disintegrated into a white cloud, swirling and rushing after another of Clive's followers. She couldn't see what was happening as the cloud expanded and thickened. Just the enemy falling from the sky to plunge into the ocean.

Neither returned as they continued after Clive and his males.

One more glance below.

Jori had finally shifted.

Dragongoddess!

He was massive.

The king never stood a chance against him.

Nor would Clive. No wonder he took flight.

Jori's jaws descended on the neck of another male trying to engage the others, snapping and clawing at Elora, who by now had gone dragon, defending herself and the others that had stood at her side.

Kolina flapped backward to avoid the male as he went sailing through the air, twisting and struggling to gain his equilibrium before he fell into the water after his friends.

Jori can't land.

Can he swim?

She hoped so.

The fighting had brought them out over the ocean and away from the coast. Kolina glanced back. Elora had returned to human form, but the enemy males were all either downed, or in flight headed toward Aeleftheria.

Elora would follow.

Kolina turned toward home.

Power and determination surged through her as she stretched her wings. Every inch of her was alive with battle-rush.

After so many years of vigilance—exhausting weeks of double patrols, the time had come.

The true attack was now.

How many are left?

In the darkness, she couldn't tell if the odds were now even. Either way, there were enough to cause devastation to the island inhabitants. If one male dragon could raze part of a sector, it wouldn't take too many more to destroy the town below the citadel if they gained that kind of proximity. The citadel was strong, but in time it too would fall.

Kymri would make it to the island to alert them.

She would find a way.

Kolina prayed to the dragon goddess as she flew, gaining speed with every push through the air.

KYMRI GLARED AT MERWIN in the tight confines of the overturned plane that had brought Jori to her.

Where he'd made love to her for the first time.

Where their love had blossomed and become bigger than themselves.

Where their child had been conceived.

Merwin sullied the precious memories, threatened the life of her child and her mate's human father, Jonathan.

Despite the situation, he maintained an air of dignity.

They were currently both bound and gagged inside the plane, invisible to any overhead patrols.

Kymri could no longer shift, even a little, with the spelled manacle locked on her wrist. She'd instructed Jonathan on where her clothing and weapon cache was on this island.

Merwin may be a dragon, but any weapon was better than no weapon. There was nowhere to escape, but Jonathan could hide in the trees. She'd assured him that Merwin wouldn't shift into his dragon again and risk exposing himself to any nearby patrols.

If he was smart. He seemed to be the smarter of the two males, but she couldn't be sure how much smarter.

Underestimating him would do neither of them any good.

Before they'd been gagged, Merwin had left them alone while he'd gone out to do whatever he was doing outside.

"Kymri, there is no point in me trying to escape and hide with a dagger that is useless against a dragon. And that's completely aside from the fact I won't leave you alone with him." *And vulnerable*, his eyes said, though he didn't say the words.

"That's not the point. You can hide and try to figure out a way to alert the patrols to our presence."

"You must know I'm not the outdoors man that Jori is."

"You're smart, you'll figure something out."

Finally, he'd given into her argument.

It didn't take long for Merwin to discover his absence, though he didn't care much, since there was no way for the professor to get off the island. Until they smelled the smoke from the fire he was trying to start.

As soon as Merwin left to find him, Kymri began to scream for him to run and hide, which led to hours of Merwin's growing frustrations as he struggled to track and contain the man before he successfully signaled any patrols.

In the end, Jonathan was recaptured and both of them were now bound and gagged so they couldn't plot anything else between them.

All they could do was try to murder him with their eyes.

It didn't work.

Below the surface of her skin, her inner dragon clawed at the magic binding, against the sensation of being trapped inside the small space. She was beginning to feel suffocated.

It was the same sort of manacle the king had used on her. Merwin had confirmed as much when she'd awakened from unconsciousness.

She also understood there was no way to get out of it unless he released her—or she killed him.

Which she would do.

If he didn't kill her and Jonathan first.

He would do it, if they became liabilities.

They almost had, with that escape and signal attempt. But at the moment they still held value as hostages. Or so he thought.

She had asked him, early on, what he was thinking. This got her a backhand and an order to shut up.

"Even if we lost and I've only ever entrapped one Aeleftherian bitch, it will be enough living with the knowledge that I have that power over you. Forever."

Swallowing her rage, she'd considered telling him he was wasting his time if he thought the citadel gates would open for him. They would never trade her life for the queen's freedom. They would never meet his demands.

But he hadn't said anything on the matter. Kept his own council.

Maybe he'd figured that out for himself.

Maybe he had a different plan.

Chapter 20

KOLINA'S HEART HAMMERED IN her chest as she flew faster and harder through the moonlit sky.

Clouds fell away as she crossed the barrier into Aeleftherian territory. The stars above her twinkled their familiar constellations seen only from this part of the world. An arched dragon with moondust wings.

She pressed on, seeking.

It wasn't the exertion that caused her heart to palpitate erratically, it was the growing terror she struggled to control.

They were getting closer to Aeleftheria.

Too close.

Where are the patrols?

Why aren't they being met by squads of guardians?

Had none of their messages made it through in time?

Nightmarish images of her peoples' homes being attacked while they slept, ripped through her mind.

Where is Kymri?

Her heart skipped several beats and she lost some altitude.

Focus. Calm.

Her altitude and speed steadied as she raced forward. She'd bypassed most of the males, ignoring the skirmishes along the way. Odson and the others engaged the males as soon as they caught up with them.

Clive is mine.

She didn't care about any of the others.

He and Merwin were the exact kind of males rallying and spreading their diseased ideas that had endangered them all for so long.

Enough.

They were echoes of their dead king. She would snuff them out.

Aeleftheria will be free of them once and for all.

A roar sounded in the distance, from the direction of Aeleftheria.

Too late. They were already there.

Oh, dragongoddess, no!

She moaned, flapping her wings furiously, pushing herself harder than she ever had in her long life. She surged past Jori and the last male dragons after Clive.

He was headed for the outermost island of the archipelago. Jori and Kymri's island.

By the time she was close enough to see the figures on the island, Clive had landed but maintained his dragon form.

She circled, assessing.

Clive stood with one clawed foot resting on the ruined body of the plane.

Merwin, in human form, watched her circle, hands on hips.

They wanted to talk.

Whatever their original plan had been, something had changed.

She circled again, Merwin dragged Jonathan from the plane into the bright moonlight. He was bound.

Kymri emerged next to him, also bound and gagged.

Rage seared through Kolina.

He'd used one of those manacles to bind Kymri's dragon.

Kolina roared.

Her instinct was to dive for him, clamp her jaws around him in a crushing embrace and drag him down to the bottom of the ocean before he could ever consider shifting.

I'm fast enough.

Clive would do the same to Kymri while you're busy with Merwin. Her dragon reminded her.

She huffed. Another rotation and Jori came into view. She waited for him and descended toward the beach, skimming the surface, then walking forward and shifted as she emerged from the water, keeping her distance.

Kymri and Jonathan were shoved back inside the dark cavity of the plane.

Following Kolina's lead, Jori rode the ocean surface to land in the shallow water, maintaining his balance, masking his inability to land properly.

He was still growling when he shifted into his human form, striding toward Merwin.

His mate and his father were at their mercy.

What was left of the Cessna wasn't strong enough to withstand the weight of a dragon.

Clive could crush them alive.

He held his stance, claws gripping the metal prison as he watched the sky for more dragons.

They arrived one by one, circling overhead, both aggressors and defenders, watching warily.

"Merwin, release them." Kolina demanded. "The queen won't be traded. Even if she wanted to, the council would never allow it."

"We aren't trading for the queen. We're trading for Mountainside's cooperation. You're going to attack the citadel and bring the queen to me."

"That didn't work the last time Kargassa tried to use me as a weapon against Aeleftheria." Jori snorted.

"No, it didn't, but the situation is different now, isn't it? No one to betray us this time. No surprises."

Movement in the dark sky above them pulled Kolina's attention. She glanced up—way, way up—and smiled.

"Are you sure about that?" Kolina said.

The light of the moon disappeared. The darkest of shadows stretched across the beach.

The wind shifted, bringing with it the scent of female dragons.

Drawn by the distracting scent, Clive looked up.

The writhing mass of shadows dove, hard and fast.

Kolina ran forward, diving into the open doorway of the plane.

"Clive!" Merwin screamed, as she scraped her limbs on her way in.

Seconds later, the metal screeched as Clive's weight began to crush it.

Kolina arched her body and began to shift into her dragon form, tearing the metal apart from within, shoving Clive up and off of them.

He scrambled back to gain his footing, striking at her with his teeth fast and hard.

She took the hits as she maintained her protective position, her steely scales blocking most of the impact.

Pain shot through her as his jaw clamped on the back of her neck and she was thrown up into the air.

Through the pain haze, she twisted, kicking her foot out, trying to catch him with her hind claws, but missed. He turned his attention back toward her vulnerable daughter and the human.

There was more fighting all around her again, like there had been on the coastal beach. Jori fended off attacks from two males, unable to reach Kymri and Jonathan.

From his blind side, Kolina dove for Clive's head, all claws extended.

I won't miss this time.

As Clive's jaws descended toward Kymri, Kolina's claws gripped the scales protecting his skull, trying to slip beneath, seeking flesh.

He roared, shaking himself to fling her off, but she held tight.

Anchored, she drew her left clawed paw back and drove it forward with all her strength, sinking the steel pointed tips into his good eye.

Now completely blind, he lashed out, stumbling.

She let go, kicking him away toward the ocean.

He continued to lash out, determined to cause as much destruction despite the loss of his sight.

She turned to Merwin, who'd shifted into dragon form and now held Kymri and Jonathan in each of his fists.

Flapping her wings, maintaining her height, she assessed how best to engage without either of the two hostages coming to harm.

Breathe in, breathe out. Think.

The battle haze receded enough for Kolina to register the change in the air surrounding them.

Above her, dragons gathered. The scent of females overlay the island as guardians swarmed, engaging the males that continued to resist.

Merwin too, looked up.

The tenor of the air changed, alive with the magic of so many dragons occupying the zone above the island.

The frequency changed, its charge thickening.

The queen.

Kolina's breath caught in her throat as Queen Regina came into view.

Wings outstretched, she glided in a circle around the combatants.

She was larger than Jori.

Glorious.

Another rotation and the attackers turned their attention to observe her.

Her magic rippled through the air, magnified by the natural magical aura that surrounded Aeleftheria.

It's been so very long since we have been graced by her dragon.

The council will be upset. Very upset.

Kolina's eyes swept the skies again.

Not just guardians. Civilian dragons too. Some with their humans riding atop them.

Pride burned through her heart.

The time had finally come. After so very long under watch and wait orders. And they were not alone. The guardians up front and center to protect their queen, people and land, as always. But allies and friends had come to help.

And their queen.

She would not sit idly back.

Regina landed with grace, the sand beneath her barely stirred as she set foot on the beach before Merwin. Her snout descended toward his, eyes locked.

The air crackled.

His head bowed away under her dominance, but he did not release his hostages.

Regina shifted to her human form.

Kolina's heart stopped. She dropped to the sand behind Regina, wings outstretched, ready to protect her queen.

Regina's hand stayed Kolina.

The queen, naked, head high, faced Merwin's dragon.

Her power continued to emanate, in rippling waves. The air writhed with it, entrancing everyone in the area.

Her focus honed in on Merwin.

Even Clive had ceased his blind thrashing and stumbling to listen to what was happening.

Regina spoke.

She did not shout, her voice augmented in such away it seemed to be cast into all of their minds.

"I can see into your mind, invader. You have something of mine. Release them."

Merwin huffed his denial.

"I sense the magic of that shackle binding my guardian's magic. I have seen this spell before. You would imprison and threaten the life of a dragon bearing a child to draw me out. Here I am. Unbind her and let them go."

Merwin growled.

"Don't you need your hands to place a shackle on me and your human mouth to recite the spell?"

It was Kolina's turn to growl, echoed by the other guardians and Aeleftherians.

In her human form, Regina was still imposing and powerful, but to a dragon's eye, less so than in her dragon form.

They all waited as Merwin considered his options.

There really weren't any.

Clive was sightless and unable to effectively help him in this moment. Their followers had ceased fighting, faced by so many opponents. And probably awed by the reality of Regina's presence.

Would he surrender?

Or would he go down fighting?

He raised his fists, still holding Kymri and Jonathan, curling his claws so that a pointed tip pressed to their chests. Neither called out for help.

Time slowed. Everyone surrounding the area was in suspension, waiting.

The queen wouldn't actually allow him to shackle her, would she?

She can't.

I will kill him.

Rage burned bright in Kolina.

This piece of dragon dung threatened her pregnant daughter, a fierce warrior in her own right, and expected to drag their queen's dignity through the mire.

Growling rumbled through her chest, expressing her displeasure.

Darting movement caught her attention from the corner of her eye, she turned in time to lash out at a male who'd decided it was an opportune time to attack. Despite her smaller size, she was able to deflect him away from her queen.

Jori swooped in to engage him before he could counter Kolina's deflection.

Some of the males took the opportunity to attack again, as though to give Merwin a chance to do whatever he was going to do.

The spell was broken.

Another wave of chaos ensued.

Regina remained as she was, waiting.

If Merwin intended to imprison her, he had to shift to human form to do it.

He dropped the human.

Jonathan fell hard, still bound as he was, but he was alive. Elora swooped in, grabbed him and removed him to safety.

That left Kymri.

Merwin had a free hand to reach for Regina, who was within his grasp.

The queen's power surged again as she focused on Merwin as he reached to grab her.

He moved slower, as though in a daze or trying to push through a barrier, Kolina couldn't discern what was happening.

Determined to grasp Regina, his grip on Kymri loosened enough that his claw was no longer pointed on her chest. He could still crush her, but the threat of impalement had slipped.

Regina shifted back into her dragon form, eye to eye with Merwin.

Her power grew exponentially. She seemed to be mesmerizing him.

Is this what Kargassa had tried to do to Jori?

Merwin's grasp slackened further, his paw fell to his side. Kymri rolled and dropped to the ground. It took her a moment to untie the rope from around her ankles and move away from the two dragons.

Although Regina's will seemed to hone in on Merwin, it also flowed out affecting Kolina and some of the others in her sphere.

Shift.

The thought, in Regina's soft voice, echoed through Kolina's mind.

She was vaguely aware of dragons landing, turning to human then just standing and waiting for Regina's next command. It was unnerving.

Clive stumbled through the trees toward the queen, human, seeking her presence.

Merwin stood entranced before her.

Free Kymri Steelscale.

Merwin turned to Kymri and uttered words—ancient words that caused the bracelet to crack.

She shook it free of her wrist.

Bind your companions and bind yourself.

Ice swept through Kolina. She'd had no idea Regina had this kind of power.

Merwin moved toward his backpack, pulled two of his shackles out and walked toward Clive. He slipped one onto his wrist, then one over his own, then the other invaders who'd been close enough to have fallen to the effects of Regina's command.

He spoke the spell.

Forget it. Forget the words to bind. Forget the words to unbind.

Forget the knowledge of this place.

This last was broadcast to all of the invaders.

Kolina shivered against the call of her power.

Even though the power was not directed at herself, she felt it.

It twisted inside of her. The unnatural dominance of another being. How terrible it must be for the target.

Jori was subjected to Kargassa's will, like this, and overcame it.

Regina swayed.

Returning to her human form, she reached out a hand seeking support. Kolina caught her, helping her stay upright.

Regina turned her face up to Kolina, giving her a weak smile of thanks. She glanced around her at all of the dragons assembled, witness to these events.

Male dragons among them.

"We should go home and give our guests a proper welcome." Regina said to Kolina.

Kolina was about to lower herself so the queen may ride her. But Regina gave her foreleg a pat and straightened herself.

Stepping back, she gave her queen room to shift into her dragon again.

With powerful legs, Regina launched herself up, catching the air with great extended wings, and guided the convoy of her guardians, citizens, and guests back to her citadel.

The prisoners were collected to be dealt with later.

This night, wounds would be tended, reports made, and thanks given to allies and friends.

Chapter 21

THE CITADEL INFIRMARY BUSTLED with those that required more serious attention after the battle.

Kolina sported salves and bandages which had been applied to a few scrapes and bruises.

Jori paced beside a curtained cot as Kymri had a full check up to insure both she and her child remained unharmed—which they both seemed to be.

"Is he alright?" Kolina asked Elora.

Elora hovered next to Jonathan's place among the shamans as they worked on the leg that had been broken when Clive dropped him on the island.

"Looks like we're taking an unscheduled, extended island vacation. The university still thinks he's at a mountain resort spending time with his son after his 'Lost in the Bermuda Triangle' debacle."

Launia, followed by Zayli, sauntered into the vast room, stopping to speak to various patients as they made their way toward Kolina and Elora.

The women smiled at one another. Elora reached out to embrace her old friend. "I suppose I'm expected to present myself to her majesty." Elora said.

Launia nodded as she released Elora and stepped back. "You are."

"She's angry."

Launia shrugged.

Elora sighed. She turned to Jonathan and kissed his brow. "I will check in on you later—if Regina doesn't throw me into a prison cell."

"Which aren't bad, as far as prisons go." Jori interjected.

"Thank you for the reassurance, darling." Elora stood on tiptoe to kiss her son's bearded cheek. To Launia, she said, "No need to go with me, I remember the way."

"Are you kidding? I wouldn't miss this."

"I'm going too," Kolina added, falling in step with both women. She cast a glance toward Jori, who gave her a wave as Zayli approached to wait with him to see Kymri.

They passed Odson, Bayn, and Carson, who lingered outside the council room.

Odson winked at Elora.

Spear-bearing guards opened the doors as they approached. The only sounds were those of their own footsteps and the swish of their loose cotton clothing.

Launia gestured toward a side door that led to the queen's council chambers.

Another door opened for them and they stepped into Regina's opulent meeting room.

She stood facing the window, back to the door, hands folded behind her.

She didn't turn until a full minute had passed after the door closed with a soft click.

Kolina's pulse increased, her shoulders tensed.

She glanced at Elora, who waited, patient and poised in the face of uncertainty.

As she always had. This was why she was the queen's ambassador.

Finally, Regina spun on her heel and faced them. Her eyes remained on Elora's face, glittering with unshed tears.

"Welcome home," she said, voice soft, gliding toward Elora, hands outstretched.

The queen pulled Elora into a hug, slowly releasing her to search her face. "We have much catching up to do, my friend."

She turned to Kolina. "Thank you for successfully completing your mission."

Kolina bowed her head in acknowledgment.

She and Launia took their leave of their sovereign so that she might spend personal time with her long-lost friend.

The doors closed behind them, and they joined Odson, Carson and Bayn, who had all remained in the hall.

She turned to Launia. "Did you have any idea the queen could do that?"

Launia shook her head. "I don't think anyone did."

"What now?" Odson asked.

Kolina shrugged as she looked from him to the other two men. "I suppose there will be some politicking going on. Decisions on the prisoners' fates. Ally agreements, what orders to send back to Marli at the mountain and all that. Who knows?"

"Won't you be participating?" Carson asked her.

Kolina glanced at Launia. "I think I will take some personal time. I have someone I want to look for."

Launia's eyes widened before a grin curved her lips upward. "Your boy."

Kolina nodded, looking at Odson. "I'm going to reach out and see what happens. It's time. Things are changing here. I can feel it."

"The queen has been...different lately." Launia said.

"She is." Kolina agreed. "Odson, I do believe I left something of value in your car. Mind if I travel back with you, after all the talk is finished here?"

"Any time, my friend. Any time. Will you wait for Kymri?"

Kolina looked back up the hall toward the infirmary as she considered Odson's question, then shook her head. "No, I will do this on my own. She has a youngling to focus on now." She turned back to Odson and smiled. "She is safe, that's all I needed to know. I will return before her child is born. But, you'll ask Jori to reinforce his internet tower, yes?"

Odson chuckled. "I shouldn't think we'd need to now that he has better control of his landings, thanks to the tips and tricks you imparted during your time with him."

Kolina reached over to shake Carson and Bayn's hands. "Thank you both. You'll be staying for a while as the queen's guests?"

Carson nodded. "I have to get back soon, I still have an open case I'm working on that we're getting close to resolving. But this is important, so I plan to be here another day or two."

"I have work waiting for me back in Toronto, but yes, as Carson said, these relations are important. It's a privilege to have been able to help Her Majesty and the Aeleftherian people." Bayn smiled and dipped his head respectfully to Kolina.

Kolina promised to meet again before it was time to leave the island.

She and Launia strode toward her private quarters. She went straight for the decanter, pouring two glasses of liquor.

Launia laughed. "It's been that kind of night."

"It's been that kind of week," she corrected with a smirk, handing Launia a cut crystal glass.

Launia sipped her drink, savoring the smoky flavor of the liquor. She swallowed and said, "You did it."

Kolina raised a brow.

"Got Elora and Kymri home safely. Routed out the evil male oppressors and brought good male allies to the queen's court. That was one hell of a successful rescue and diplomatic mission, Kolina."

Kolina coughed on her drink, laughing. "If that's what you'd call that mess—I'll take it." She took another sip of her drink. "It was more of a fly by the seat of my pants and hope like hell I don't fuck it all up, kind of...adventure." She said.

"But you did it." Launia emphasized the point of her success.

"There came a point I really wasn't sure any of this would work out. I'm sure Kymri won't stay, and I think I've accepted that. As I'm sure Her Majesty will very likely have to accept that Elora will also leave."

"And you?"

Kolina's gaze dropped to her glass, swirling the liquid again and again.

When she finally looked up to meet her friend's eyes, her vision blurred.

She blinked and drew a deep breath.

"I have some things to think about. Maybe some personal changes are in my future." She knocked back the rest of her drink. "I'm going to look for my son and try to reconnect with him."

"Do you think he'll be open to it?" Launia asked, her voice heavy with empathy.

"Expect the worst, hope for the best." Kolina shrugged. "I have to at least try, right?"